WHAT BLOGGERS ARE SA

MIND OF A KILLER

A HISTORICAL NOVEL BY

AMY CECIL

This book will turn you around every which way. Getting into the mind of the Ripper takes guts and nerves of steel. Amy does this while keeping you guessing. The foreboding feeling flows from the pages into you.

Leave Me Be I'm Reading

There is a fine line between love and hate and Amy Cecil has managed to write it on both ends. I was literally gob smacked at the outcome of this book.

Alison Pridie Blog

Amy Cecil sure knows how to pull you in with the very first Chapter. Marie is dead and they're still looking for Jack the Ripper. This book is intriguing, captivating and painfully beautiful!

Elaine and Tami's JB3 Blackbirds

Amy Cecil has brought the twisted mind of the Ripper to a new level. The spirit of his beloved helps Jax along the way to find the true killer. Find out for yourself if he finds the Ripper. But, be warned, you will not be able to set this book down once you start. A thriller that will leave you breathless as you try to unravel the mystery.

A Little Book Love

If Ripper left you wanting more, then The Mind of a Killer will leave you on the floor begging for mercy. A beautifully written sequel, deserving of its name. Cecil delivers and perfectly pairs suspense with drama to ensnare the reader within a timeless mystery.

BAMM PR & Blog Services

Suggested reading order in the Ripper Series

Ripper

Mind of a Killer

Mind of a Killer

A Historical Novel By
Amy Cecil

The Mind of a Killer – Ripper Series Book 2 – Amy Cecil

Copyright © 2019 Amy Cecil

All rights reserved in accordance with the U.S. Copyright Act of 1976. The scanning, uploading, and electronic sharing of any part of this book without the permission of the author constitutes unlawful piracy and theft of the author's intellectual property. If you would like to use materials from this book (other than for review purposes), prior written permission must be obtained by contacting the author.

FBI Anti-Piracy Warning: The unauthorized reproduction or distribution of a copyrighted work is illegal. Criminal copyright infringement, including infringement without monetary gain, is investigated by the FBI and is punishable by up to five years in federal prison along with a fine of $250,000.

This is a work of fiction. Names, characters, businesses, places, events, and incidents are either the products of the author's imagination or used in a fictitious manner. Any resemblance to actual persons living or dead, or actual events, is purely coincidental or used in a fictitious manner. The author acknowledges that all song titles, film titles, film characters, and novels mentioned in this book are the property of and belong to their respective owners.

Any views expressed in this book are fictitious and not necessarily the views of the author.

Thank you for your support of the author's rights.

Book cover design by Rebecca Garcia of Dark Wish Designs.
www.darkwishdesigns.com

Book layout and formatting by Ellie Bockert Augsburger of Creative Digital Studios
www.creativedigitalstudios.com

Editing Services provided by Angie Wade of Novel Nurse Editing.
www.novelnurseeditng.com.

ISBN- 9781700455901

DEDICATION

This book is dedicated to the members of my reader group, Amy's Amazing Street Girls. You ladies are amazing, and I am so blessed to have you all in my life. Thank you for all you do for me!

AUTHOR'S NOTE

Please be advised that this book contains subjects and graphic content that may be considered dark, taboo, and/or disturbing. If you are a reader who is sensitive to certain triggers and graphic murder descriptions, then perhaps this may not be the book for you. You've been warned.

PROLOGUE

Inside the mind of a serial killer ...

They will never catch me, I think as I sit here in this God-awful room waiting for her to return home. I know she will. How do I know this? I know this because everything I've done until this point has assured me she will return here on this night to face her fate.

Jackson Kent. I scoff. He was nothing but a puppet in my grand performance, and soon, he will be a victim. It was me who made sure they met in the alleyway the night I killed Mary Ann Nichols. It was me who made sure Mr. Kent was away when Annie Chapman, Catherine Eddowes, and Elizabeth Stride were murdered. You ask how?

Well, I shall tell you.

Victoria Kent is a dear friend and a regular client of mine. She has been under my control for months. I manipulated her episodes so that they would occur at the same times as the murders of the first four women.

I also methodically planned each murder location so that they were closing in on Miller's Court. I wanted Marie to see I was closing in on her. I believe I was quite obvious. I'll be surprised if she didn't see it coming.

I murdered her friend, Elizabeth Stride. Brilliant on my part. I deserve a pat on the back for that one.

But the best manipulation of all was the handwriting. One of my most clever and calculated moves, if I have to say so myself. One afternoon as Mr. Kent was leaving the House of Lords, I approached him and asked him for directions. The clever part was when I asked him to write them down. Then, with a sample of his handwriting, I worked on mastering his penmanship. Once I was satisfied with my forgery, I submitted a letter to: The Boss, Central News Office. I knew that with her living in Kent's home, she would see his handwriting at some point once my letter was public information. And I knew the police, Scotland Yard, and the press could not keep the letter quiet. I played them all perfectly.

I am so pleased with myself.

I pull the knife from my cloak. Its silver shines in the candlelight, and I revel in the feel of such an instrument. I run my finger ever so lightly along the knife's edge to feel its sharpness. *This will do nicely,* I think to myself. Placing it carefully back into my cloak, I wait.

I'm an actor on a stage, each murder a performance that outshines the last. Tonight will be my encore. The mutilations I have planned for Miss Kelly far exceed any of those performed on the other women. They were practice, stepping stones I set up to prepare me for this last show. She will know this was all for her. She will know these women died because of her. She will feel my pain, and she will die.

Several minutes go by and then I see her small, frail hand reach through the window to unlatch the door. She's here. My heart races. The blood pulsing through my body in anticipation of what's about to happen causes my dick to grow hard and persistent with want.

She opens the door slowly, and I see surprise and shock on her face. She knows who I am, and she knows why I am here.

"What are you doing here?" she asks.

I rise from the chair and approach her. "I've come for you," I reply. I see no fear on her face, as if she was expecting this. Surely, she had to know. After everything that happened between us, she had to know I would come for her and make her pay for my heartache.

"Are you..." She stumbles over her words.

"You want to know if I'm the Ripper?" I reply, pulling my knife out from my cloak. "What do you think, Marie?"

"And you have come for me?" she asks.

I try not to laugh at her question. Is she serious?

"I thought you—"

"Surely you knew you would be next." I've had enough of her stalling, and the absurdity of this line of questions irritates me.

"But it has been over a month since the last victim!" she cries, as if it will save her. "Why murder more when you've gotten away with it?" I see confusion on her face. "Why didn't you just come for me in the first place?"

I chuckle. "A serial killer never stops killing until he is caught. You've known that all along." I pause and then say, "Besides, stopping would ruin all the fun."

"Fun?" she questions. "You call these murders fun? Those poor women. How could you?"

"Oh, Marie, you surprise me. You knew I wouldn't stop, and you knew I'd be coming for you. Didn't you? Deep down in the depths of your soul, you've always known it was me. You questioned, you doubted, you even accused an innocent man unjustly. But deep down, you knew. That's why you kept coming back here. Subconsciously, you came to find me. Somehow you knew I would eventually be waiting right here for you."

Her shoulders slump, and defeat is written all over her face. Ah yes, the submission gives me the greatest high. She is now mine.

"Now be a good girl and let me do what I came here to do. I need you to make this easy, Marie. Submit to me," I say calmly. I am surprised to see a twinge of defiance on her face.

"What if I don't?" she asks.

"Marie, you know better than to play power games with me. You know all I have to do is command you, and like the good little pet you are, you will obey." I pause, waiting for a reaction. When there is none, I continue. "Lie on the bed, Marie." Without any hesitation, she does as she's told. Seeing her give up control makes me feel like a god. I can bend her to my will; I have all the control. Now my grand performance can begin.

"Anything you want to say before you can no longer talk?"

"I'm sorry for all the pain I caused you."

I'm sorry for you, Marie. You could have saved so many lives if you had said that a long time ago. It's a shame you were selfish, headstrong, and didn't care about consequences. It's refreshing to see you show some sign of remorse in the end. It's a pity that it's too late.

I take the knife and slash her throat.

Marie bleeds from her jugular as I continue to prepare the canvas of her murder. When I am done, I admire the work of art before me. It's my best work.

I leave the scene, her heart safely wrapped and tucked in my pocket. It's an odd thing to have in one's pocket, but I did say her heart would be mine, and now it is.

My work here is done. It's time for me to leave Whitechapel.

CHAPTER ONE

November 10, 1888

JACKSON KENT

The newspaper headlines this morning leave me devastated. My heart has been obliterated and lies in fragments all over the floor. Marie has been found, but there won't be any chances of returning her home. The Ripper got to her before I could.

He destroyed her.

He mutilated her.

She is dead.

The walls around my heart turn to steel. I told myself I would never love again and then she came along. I couldn't help myself. She brought me back to life.

After I read the disheartening news of the day, I fold my newspaper and lay it on the table. The hurt and despair consume me. I cry. I holler. I curse. *Fuck, fuck, fuck! If only you could have trusted me, Marie!*

I tried to save her. I searched and searched for her, but she was always one step ahead of me. She ran right into the arms of the killer.

"Sir, are you unwell?" Rothschild asks hesitantly as he walks into the dining room.

"I know what happened to Marie." My shoulders slump as the realization of what's happened truly hits me. *She's gone.*

"Sir?" Rothschild takes a step toward me.

"The Ripper got her." I pick up the paper and hand it to him. "He mutilated her beautiful face and body."

Rothschild takes the paper from me.

"He fucking cut out her heart, Rothschild. He fucking took her heart." I bring my hands to my face as the tears begin to flow again.

Rothschild opens the paper and begins to read.

I wipe the tears from my eyes. "Brace yourself. It's terribly gruesome."

Times (London)
Saturday, November 10, 1888

ANOTHER WHITECHAPEL MURDER

During the early hours of yesterday morning, another murder of a most revolting and fiendish character took place in Spitalfields. This is the seventh which has occurred in this immediate neighbourhood, and the character of the mutilations leaves very little doubt that the murderer in this instance is the same person who committed the previous ones, with which the public is fully acquainted.

The scene of this last crime is at 26 Dorset Street, Spitalfields, which is about 200 yards from 29 Hanbury Street, where the previous victim Annie Chapman was so foully murdered. The victim's name is Mary Jane Kelly, though she also went by Mary Jane or Marie Kelly. The entrance to her room at 26 Dorset Street is up a narrow court, in which are some half-a-dozen houses, and which is known as Miller's Court; it is entirely separated from the other portion of the house, and has an entrance leading into the court...

> *A horrible and sickening sight presented itself. The poor woman lay on her back on the bed, entirely naked. Her throat was cut from ear to ear, right down to the spinal column. The ears and nose had been cut clean off. The breasts had also been cleanly cut off and placed on a table which was at the side of the bed. The stomach and abdomen had been ripped open, while the face was slashed about so that the features of the poor creature were beyond all recognition. The kidneys had also been removed from the body and placed on the table by the side of the breasts. The liver had likewise been removed and laid on the right thigh. The lower portion of the body and the uterus had been cut out and appeared to be missing. The thighs had been cut. The heart of the victim had also been removed but was never found.*
>
> *A more horrible or sickening sight could not be imagined. The clothes of the woman were lying by the side of the bed, as though they had been taken off and laid down in an ordinary manner. While this examination was being made, the photographer who had been sent for arrived and took photographs of the body, the organs, the room, and its contents.*
>
> *There was no appearance of a struggle having taken place, and, although a careful search of the room was made, no knife or instrument of any kind was found ...*[i]

Rothschild takes a deep breath. "Oh good Lord." He sighs and sets the paper on the table. "So what do you plan to do?"

His question surprises me. I look up at him. "Why would you ask that? There's nothing I can do, Rothschild. She's dead."

He pulls out the seat next to me. "May I?"

"Of course, you know we are well beyond formalities here."

He sits down. "Sir, I ask because if it were me..." He picks up the paper and lays it in front of me, the ghastly headline blaring at me. "And the woman I loved was brutally murdered in this way, I'd want answers. I'd want to catch the man who did this and castrate him. I'd want to kill him."

"I want all those things, Rothschild, but nobody knows who he is. He has baffled everyone, including the Metropolitan police."

"But sir, the police, though it is sad to say, do not have the means and connections that you do. You have friends at Scotland Yard." He glances down at the paper. "Actually, I remember reading that Frederick Abberline was pulled from Scotland Yard and sent back to H Division. You and he go way back."

"That's right, I remember reading that as well."

"Seems to me the perfect in for you to get information."

I look at him curiously. "My instincts tell me you've got some pretty specific ideas about this whole Ripper thing. Let's hear it."

"Well, I have been reading everything printed about these murders. Each murder gets more and more gruesome, with Marie's being even more horrific than the last." He gets up from the chair and paces. "I feel as if there is some type of connection between these five women. Something or someone has pushed this killer to do this and to do it with these specific women."

He stops pacing.

"So you think if I find a connection between them, I will find the killer?" I ask.

"Perhaps, but let's take this a step further. Did you notice you were tending to Victoria during every single murder, beginning with Polly Nichols? Well, except for Marie's, but you were not home as you were searching for her. Did you happen to take into account that the very night you met Marie, a murder had just occurred? Didn't you meet Elizabeth Stride, a friend of Marie's?"

I never gave much thought about the things Rothschild just mentioned, but as I contemplate them, understanding emerges and I realize he is onto something. I did meet Marie the night Polly

Nichols was murdered; I was rushing because I had received a tip on Victoria. And yes, I was tending to Victoria the night Annie Chapman was murdered, as well as the nights Elizabeth Stride and Catherine Eddowes were murdered. Marie believed I was the Ripper, not once but twice. The first time I was able to show her I was not. The second time, I did not get the chance, although I tried to find her.

The Ripper will not murder again because Marie was his intended last victim. He knew her. Now I realize Marie was the reason for all this, and I was just his pawn. He intended to split us up, making me look like a killer. He fucking set me up. I take a deep breath. "Oh my God."

"You see it, don't you?" Rothschild sits again.

"I do. This was all about her."

"I think so." He lays his hand on my arm in a caring gesture. "And I think you have the means, the connections, and your brief history with Marie to catch him once and for all."

"I don't even know her surname. I never asked because... well, we were just getting to know each other. It never mattered."

He grabs the paper and hands it to me. "Yes, you do."

I look at the paper and begin to read the article again.

> *The scene of this last crime is at 26 Dorset Street, Spitalfields, which is about 200 yards from 29 Hanbury Street, where the previous victim Annie Chapman was so foully murdered. The victim's name is Mary Jane Kelly, though she also went by Mary Jane or Marie Kelly.*

"You have a place to start." He gets up from the chair and says, "Now the only question that remains is what are you going to do about it?"

"I'm going to find out more about Mary Jane or Marie Kelly. And then, I'm going to catch a killer."

Chapter Two

After my discussion with Rothschild, I finish my tea and proceed to my study. I walk over to my desk, pull out some parchment, and sit. After wetting my quill, I make a list of all the places and people who knew Marie. *Madame Grace, Julia, Dom from the Princess Anne, and Joe. Yes, Joe Barnett.* I circle Joe's name. Who do I know at Scotland Yard? *Frederick Abberline and Edmund Reid.* Abberline was at Scotland Yard, but after Polly Nichols, he was transferred back to J Division. Edmund has been with H Division and has been assisting in the case. The inquisition is scheduled for Monday. I should probably wait until the inquisition because they both will have acquired as much as they could beforehand.

The next day, the notice for the inquisition is posted in the *Star*. It's scheduled for ten o'clock this very morning. I'll start there and then I'll pay a visit to my old friend, Frederick Abberline.

I ring for Rothschild, and in no time he's entering my study. "You rang, sir?"

"Yes, Rothschild, could you please have Carlton prepare my carriage." I rise from the desk, take the piece of parchment that contains my list from yesterday, and walk to the door. "We're taking a trip to Whitechapel."

Rothschild grins, and I can tell he is pleased. He is certain I should be doing this, and I have to say I agree. Him pointing out my connections with the Scotland Yard and the House of Lords could prove most helpful in catching the Ripper. At least I am now hopeful. Yesterday I was wallowing in my sorrows, but now I feel refreshed with a purpose. I know I can't bring Marie back—that Chapter is officially closed—but perhaps I can find justice for the five women who lost their lives at the hands of this sick man, Jack the Ripper.

Knowing I need to make myself fit in while visiting Whitechapel, I make my way upstairs to change my attire to something less formal. People will be more forthcoming if I appear to be one of them. By the time I return downstairs, Carlton is waiting at the door.

"Your carriage is ready, sir." He offers a slight bow. "Where will we be going?"

"First, Shoreditch Town Hall. We need to be there by ten, doable?" I found it odd that the inquest was not being held in Whitechapel, but I presume the police and the coroner have their reasons.

"Yes, sir, that should not be a problem."

"Good, then we will go to H Division of the Metropolitan Police. If it is still light afterward, Madame Grace's brothel and possibly Miller's Court," I say as I walk past him and out the front door.

"Very good, sir," he says as he follows me out the door.

The carriage arrives at the town hall about five minutes before ten. Perfect timing. "We've arrived, sir." Carlton says as he turns back to face me.

I chuckle. "I can see that, Carlton. And thank you for getting us here in time."

He gets down from his post and opens the carriage door. I step out and proceed to the entrance.

I walk inside and am surprised by the number of people who are in attendance. I recognize some, such as Inspector Frederick Abberline, Superintendent T. Arnold, Coroner George Bagster Phillips, and his deputy, Mr. Hodgekin.

The proceedings begin with the jury introductions. One juror is annoyed and asks why they were there because the murder did not happen in Shoreditch. The coroner's officer, Mr. Hodgekin, snaps at the juror stating they know what they are doing and it is not the jury's place to question. A small argument ensues until the jury has no further objections. He never really gives a reason other than the fact Shoreditch is his district and jurisdiction lies where the body lies, not where it was murdered. The jury is then duly sworn in.

Inspector Abberline proceeds by explaining that the jury has viewed the body before it was coffined, as well as Marie's room where the murder took place. *I wonder if he will allow me to view the same.* Once all the semantics are out of the way, the depositions begin.

I listen intently while witness after witness speaks about Marie. Some knew her very well, but others are minor acquaintances. One I recognize by face and name: Joseph Barnett, who lived with Marie for eight months. I can't help the twinge of jealousy I feel as he talks about her intimately. He loved her, and she chose me. She had never loved him, and the last time I saw him, he was a broken man.

Hours pass as the many witnesses talk about Marie's last night.

After neighbors and friends give their testimonies, George Bagster Phillips gets up to speak. He describes the room, the blood, and how he found Marie. He doesn't go into a lot of detail—I guess to spare those in attendance—but all the specifics will be in his report. He states in conclusion that "The large quantity of blood under the bedstead, the saturated condition of the palliasse, pillow, and sheet at the top corner of the bedstead nearest to the partition leads me to the conclusion that the severance of the right carotid artery was the immediate cause of death. It was inflicted while the deceased was lying at the right side of the bedstead and her head and neck in the top right-hand corner."

I close my eyes and try to envision the horrific picture he describes. *Oh God, Marie, what did he do to you?*

When the coroner finishes, he asks the jury if they have any questions. Since there are none, the hearing adjourns for a short break. I want to speak with Frederick during the break, but he disappears into the back offices.

After the break, the testimonies continue, and by the time they are done, it is well after six o'clock. It is concluded that the jury has quite sufficient evidence before them upon which to give a verdict.

The coroner asks, "What is the verdict?"

The foreman stands and replies, "Willful murder, against some person or persons unknown."

Well I am not surprised; it is obvious it was willful murder. I shrug. All that time to determine Marie was murdered... Such a waste of time in my opinion.

I step outside and am disappointed to see it is already getting dark. Frederick has had a long day. I decide I will not bother him today and come back tomorrow. He should have the inquisition report by then as well.

Carlton is waiting for me. "Where to, sir?" he asks.

"Home, Carlton. It's late, and it's been a long day." I look up at the sky. "It looks like rain."

"It does, sir, but hopefully we will beat the rain home." He opens the carriage door. "Will we be returning tomorrow?"

"Yes," I say as I step inside. He returns to his post and we are off. My mind wanders back to the testimonies I heard earlier. So many people had seen Marie and some had even spoken with her. Some saw her with another man, of varying descriptions. Many said they heard her singing and that her spirits were good. Was she happy?

I think back to my conversation with Jasper. He was Marie's coachman and was the last person to see her from my household. From what he said, she was scared. So why was she singing? And then it occurs to me. Many said she was drunk. It makes me so sad. I never gave much thought to how a person would spend their last night alive. How could any of us have known we would never see her again? I had been so sure I would find her and make everything right.

I know she was running. She was in fear of her life because of me. Jasper told me everything and how he tried to stop her. I cannot fault him. A woman like Marie cannot be stopped once her mind is made up. Her death was horrific and gruesome, and I hate that for her. If I only I could have found her in time. But I obviously did not. The only thing easing my mind in all this is Marie died knowing without a doubt that I was not the Ripper.

Carlton pulls up in front of the house, and once we are stopped, I exit the carriage and make my way inside. Rothschild greets me as I enter the house. "Good evening, sir," he says as he takes my coat.

"Rothschild, thank you." I am exhausted. The testimonies today have taken their toll on me. My head hurts. "Please tell Cook I will have my dinner upstairs in my private parlor." I begin to walk toward the stairs. "And have her send up some powder for my head."

"Very well, sir."

I walk up the stairs and make my way to my bedchamber. When I get to the end of the hall, I pause and glance into Marie's room. The bed is neatly made, and there is no sign anyone was staying in it only two days ago. A tear slides down my cheek. If only she would have waited to talk to me. *If only.*

CHAPTER THREE

I wake the next morning anxious. My sleep was filled with horrible nightmares of Marie and her murder. In every one of them, the killer was there. I could feel I knew him, but I could never get a look at his face. It is unnerving and makes me more determined to find the son of a bitch.

"Sir?" Rothschild asks as I sit for breakfast. "If I may, how did it go yesterday?"

I look up at him curiously. "I'm surprised you didn't ask last night when I got home." I chuckle.

"Well, sir, I wanted to, but you looked as if you had fought a battle and lost. I thought it best to let you rest."

I nod. "Good thinking. And you are right. I felt as if I had been beaten. It was a long day filled with testimony of those who saw Marie in the last hours of her life. The coroner gave his report, and it was deemed willful murder by someone unknown." I take a sip of my tea. "When the inquisition was over, it was too late to go to H Division. Today I will be visiting Frederick Abberline. Hopefully the trip will afford me more information."

"Indeed. I hope it does."

"I intend to visit Madame Grace as well. I am hoping she will be able to help me find Joseph Barnett. I definitely would like to hear more from him." I take another sip of my tea and the last bite of my pudding, wipe my mouth with my napkin, and stand. "Please tell Carlton I will be ready at half past."

Rothschild nods, and I walk past him to leave the dining room.

***

Thirty minutes later, I am in the carriage on my way to H Division in Whitechapel. I am eager to speak with Inspector Abberline. Frederick is an old friend, and lucky for me, just like Rothschild said, he was brought back to H Division in September to take the lead on the Whitechapel murders. Last year, he had been promoted out of the district, but his unrivaled knowledge of the area and its criminal underworld sent him back to take charge of the investigation into the murders.

I met Frederick several years ago at a fundraiser. I remember him to be a portly and gentle-speaking man. We were fast friends. Over the years, I confided in him about Victoria and her escapades. He was pleased to help and has been the one who has kept an eye on her. He is my informant whenever she is involved in something untoward.

Knowing his abilities and his knowledge of crime and criminals in the East End, frankly I am surprised the Ripper has not been caught. But I am confident the elusiveness of the murderer is about to change.

I'm hoping he will understand my story and provide me with the information I need to catch Ripper. I know, I know, it's presumptuous for me to think I will catch him. After all, they've been trying to catch him for a couple months now with not one solid lead. What makes me think I will be different?

It is different because this is personal. I am sure I know the Ripper personally. I may not know him well or at first sight, but he made me a pawn in his reign of terror, and I am convinced I have met him at least once in my life. Secondly, he made this personal when he took Marie from me. He knew her before me, of that I am sure. I am also sure every murder he committed was his way of getting one step closer to Marie. This whole thing has been about her. And thirdly, he wants me to find him. He wants me to know who he is and his connection to Marie. He wants me to know why he killed all those innocent women. And more importantly, he wants to kill me too.

An hour later, we arrive at H Division. Once inside, a young officer greets me. "Can I help you, sir?"

I look down at the young man sitting at the desk and take note of the name on pinned to his lapel. "Dew, is it?"

"Yes, sir, Walter Dew."

"Very good, Walter Dew, I shall like to see Inspector Frederick Abberline."

"I'm terribly sorry, sir, but Mr. Abberline is very busy and is not seeing visitors. There is a killer roaming the streets of Whitechapel, and I'm afraid it takes up the majority of his time. Perhaps once this monster is—"

"Officer Dew," I say, interrupting him. "Please tell Mr. Abberline that Jackson Kent is here to see him. And, tell him it is urgent. I have pertinent information on Mary Jane Kelly."

At the mention of Marie's name, the young officer perks up and stands. "Of course, sir. I will get him straight away." He rushes off, and a few minutes later, Frederick comes walking toward me.

"Jax! Good to see you, old friend." He holds out his hand, and I shake it graciously. "Come, let's talk in my office." He puts his arm around my shoulders and guides me to his office. Once inside, he says, "Take a seat."

I sit in the chair across from his desk as he sits in the chair behind it.

"Officer Dew tells me you have information on Mary Jane Kelly?"

I nod. "I do, but first I must tell you I have an ulterior motive for being here. My plan is to catch the Ripper."

He laughs. "Jax, we don't know who he is. You could get yourself killed." He gets up from his chair, walks to the other side of his desk, and leans on the front. "You really need to let the police handle the investigation."

"I cannot do that, Frederick." I put my hands over my face, then rub at the growth on my chin. "You see, Mary Jane Kelly was the woman I have been seeing for the past two and somewhat-half months."

The look of astonishment that surfaces on his face does not surprise me. I am sure it is the last thing he expected to hear. Without allowing him to utter another word, I tell him my story. He listens intently, only stopping to ask for clarification at times. When I finish, he gives a heavy sigh.

"Holy fuck, Jax." He takes a deep breath. "Well, that explains why you were present at the inquisition yesterday. I had been wondering why you were there. I had wanted to speak with you, but everything got so hectic, I did not get a chance. I'm sorry."

I wave my hand. "I totally understand." I sigh. "So now you know why it's personal. I know this man. I may not know his name or what he looks like at the moment, but I know him. I've encountered him at least once, and I can assure you with your help, I will have him identified within the next few weeks."

"You know I could lose my job if anyone found out I was giving you confidential information about the case?"

I get up from the chair and pace. "I know, but think of the hero you would be if you caught the guy."

He grins, and I know I've got him.

"Think about the headlines, Fred," I say encouragingly. His ego will not be able to pass up the opportunity to catch the Ripper. "So…" I lean over his desk eagerly. "Tell me what you know."

He looks at me and takes a deep breath. "Where to start?" he asks, defeated. He's desperate. He wants this case solved. He wants to be the hero, and after five women having been brutally murdered, he has no other choice but to take all the help he can get. "As you know, I have fourteen years' experience in this district. When the murders began, I was at the central office at Scotland Yard. Because of my experience and knowledge of Whitechapel and the surrounding areas—the people and the businesses—upon the application of Superintendent Arnold, I came back to Whitechapel as chief of the detective corps right before Annie Chapman was murdered." He begins to pace. "I gave myself up to study the Polly

Nichols murder, and subsequently, the three women who were brutally murdered after. But when I walked into 13 Millers Court two days ago, nothing prepared me for the horrific mess the Ripper had left. Phillips's testimony yesterday did not do it justice." He shakes his head in disgust.

"Tell me?" I plead.

"You loved Ms. Kelly?"

I nod. "I did."

He shakes his head again. "Then I mustn't tell you. It will never leave your mind, and you do not want to remember her like that."

I walk back to his desk. "Fred, I have to know. I have to know everything he did to her if I am ever going to catch him."

He rakes his hand through the very little hair he has on his head. "When I was first contacted about the situation at Miller's Court, I sent a telegram to Sir Charles Warren to bring in bloodhounds. It was the first murder that happened inside a dwelling, and I had hoped that with the help of the bloodhounds they could have picked up on the killer's scent or something. After the telegram was sent, I made my way to Miller's Court. I arrived around eleven thirty that morning and waited. I wanted the bloodhounds to enter first. I waited until half past one when Superintendent Arnold arrived and informed me that the order for the bloodhounds had been countermanded." He stopped and looked at me, and I could tell by his expression he truly wanted to spare me from hearing what he had to say next.

"We then forced the door open and stepped inside."

I think about his words. Why on earth would they need to force the door open? Did the killer lock the door behind him? And if he did, why? Why would he do that? Something doesn't add up. "You forced the door?"

He stumbles. "Uh, yeah? The door to Kelly's room was locked." He looks down at the papers on his desk and then back at me. "There was a section of the front window that was broken out. I guess we could have reached in and unlocked the door. I never really gave it much thought."

"Do you not find it odd the door was locked?"

He shakes his head. "Frankly, I did not even think about it because of the broken window. I assumed he got in that way."

"Then why did you not go in that way as well?"

He shakes his head again. "I do not know."

This is disconcerting to me that Fred does not find it odd her door was locked, especially since anyone could enter from the broken section of the window, including the police. I remember when we were at her flat just a few days ago. Marie had told Barnett it was over and that she loved me. She thanked him for all he had done for her and we left. As we were walking out, we heard the sound of glass breaking and looked back. Barnett had thrown something at the window, which is how the window broke. Although I believe that Marie knew him, anyone could have entered her flat through the window. Marie and I left a broken man that morning, and I found myself feeling sorry for him. I tuck these thoughts away in the back of my mind. "So, you broke down the door and entered her room. What did you see?"

Tears well in his eyes. "Jax you can't even begin to imagine."

"Unfortunately, Fred, I can. Please go on." I fidget in my chair and cross my legs. On the outside, I am strong and ready to hear all the disturbing details. Inside, I am gutted and praying I can get through this conversation without breaking down.

"As we walked into the room, the remains of Miss Kelly were lying on the bed located opposite the door. A fire fierce enough to melt the solder between a kettle and its spout had burnt in the grate. Based on the remains, it appeared it was fueled with clothing. My guess is they grabbed some things lying around and burnt them to give sufficient light for the murderer to do his work. The clothes she was wearing were probably the ones neatly folded and placed to the side." He smirks. "I had the unenviable task of sifting through the ashes in the hopes that we could yield any clues, which we did not."

He hesitates.

"What else?" I ask anxiously. He's proceeding with caution, and I just want him to throw it out there. I know it has to be gruesome, but I'm prepared. I have to be if I am ever going to get justice for Marie and the other women who were brutally murdered.

"Jax, it was horrific. There was blood everywhere." He pulls a file off the stack on his desk and sets it down in front of him. "Do you really want to know all the details?"

"Fred, I told you. I need to know everything. Every horrific detail."

He opens the file and pulls out a sheet of paper and hands it to me across the desk. "Here is Phillips's and Bonds's postmortem report on Miss Kelly. I know you heard some of this yesterday, but this is the full report."

I take the paper from him and glance at it. When I glance back at him, he nods.

"Everything you want to know about her murder and what that sick bastard did to her is in that report."

I sit back in the chair and read.

The body was lying naked in the middle of the bed, the shoulders flat but the axis of the body inclined to the left side of the bed. The head was turned onto the left cheek. The left arm was close to the body with the forearm flexed at a right angle and lying across the abdomen. The right arm was slightly abducted from the body and rested on the mattress. The elbow was bent, the forearm supplying with the fingers clenched. The legs were wide apart, the left at a right angle to the trunk and the right forming an obtuse angle with the pubis.

The whole of the surface of the abdomen and thighs was removed, and the abdominal cavity emptied of viscera. The breasts were cut off, the arms mutilated by several jagged wounds, and the face hacked beyond recognition of the features. The tissues of the neck were severed all round, down to the bone.

The viscera were found in various parts visible: the uterus and kidneys with one breast under the head, the other breast by the right foot, the liver between the feet, the intestines by the right side, and the spleen by the left side of the body. The flaps removed from the abdomen and thighs were on the table.

The bed clothing at the right corner was saturated with blood, and on the floor beneath was a pool of blood covering about 2 ft. square. The wall by the right side of the bed and then a line near the neck was marked by blood which had struck it in several places.

The face was gashed in all directions—the nose, cheeks, eyebrows, and ears being partly removed. The lips were blanched and cut by several incisions running obliquely down to the chin. There are also numerous cuts extending irregularly across all features.

The neck was cut through the skin and other tissues right down to the vertebrae, the fifth and sixth being deeply notched. The skin cuts in the front of the neck show distinct ecchymosis. The air passage was cut at the lower part of the larynx through the cricoid cartilage.

Both breasts were more or less removed by circular incisions, with muscle down to the ribs being attached to the breast. The intercostals between the fourth, fifth, and sixth ribs were cut through, the contents of the thorax visible through the openings.

> *The skin and tissues of the abdomen from the coastal arch to the pubis were removed in three large flats. The right thigh was denuded in front to the bone. The flap of skin, including the external organs of generation and part of the right buttock were detached. The left thigh was stripped of skin facia and muscles as far as the knee.*
>
> *The left calf showed a long gash through skin and tissues to the deep muscles in reaching from the knee to 5 inches above the ankle. Both arms and forearms had extensive jagged wounds.*
>
> *The right thumb showed a small superficial incision about 1 inch long, with extravasation of blood in the skin, and there were several abrasions on the back of the hand, moreover showing the same condition.*
>
> *On opening the thorax, it was found that the right lung was minimally adherent by old firm adhesions. The lower part of the lung was broken and torn away. The left lung was intact. It was adherent at the apex, and there were a few adhesions along the side. In the substances of the lung, there was several nodules of consolidation.*
>
> *The pericardium was open below, and the heart absent. In the abdominal cavity, there was some partly digested food and fish and potatoes, and similar food was found in the remains of the stomach attached to the intestines.*[ii]

I place the paper on Frederick's desk and attempt to take a deep breath, but I can't. The air is stuck inside my lungs, until I gasp. My chest is heavy and I'm struggling. It takes everything in me to breathe. "Good Lord," I say, though it was barely audible. My stomach turns as bile rises in my throat. My heart aches as the realization of what she endured settles itself inside my mind. How does one benefit by doing such things to another human being? Is it possible for the mind to convince you into thinking mutilating a person is gratifying? Is it possible to have any sort of mind at all when you commit such inhumane acts?

"I warned you."

I shake my head. "I knew he mutilated her. I read the papers. I heard the testimony. But you are right, they only scraped the surface." I glance at the paper again. "Were the other murders like this?"

"No, which is strange. The mutilation of Kelly was by far the most extensive. It was the only murder that did not occur on the streets, so he had more time considering he was in the privacy of her room. He must have known her because there wasn't even an indication of forced entry into her room, as you already know. She let him in, or he came in through the broken window." Well, that explains why he was not concerned about having to break down the door. Fred thinking the same as me is good. It makes my theory more viable, and I feel more confident I am heading down the correct path. "Her death tells me this is personal, not just some random prostitute on the streets as the others appeared."

I nod. "I agree. That's been my thought since the murder. In fact, I would bet money on the fact that he knew her."

"Both Dr. Phillips and Dr. Bond determined, based on their examination, that Kelly died approximately twelve hours prior, with a time of death window between two and eight in the morning." He shuffles through some papers in the file in front of him and then says, "They also believe her throat was cut first and all the remaining mutilations happened postmortem and took the Ripper at least two to three hours to complete."

Oh, thank God! At least she did not suffer through all his mutilations. The slash to the throat would be quick, blood would have spilled from her throat, and she may have gagged a little but would have died rather quickly compared to being tortured by a knife over and over.

"The papers indicate it may be a person who possesses medical training. Do you agree?"

"I did at first, but after speaking with Bond and Phillips, they believe—and I have to agree—the murderer did not have any medical knowledge. It is clear the mutilations were not inflicted by a person who had any scientific or anatomical knowledge. These women were butchered. A surgeon would be precise."

"Where are her remains now? May I see her?" I really don't know why I even asked this. There's nothing left to see. But a part of me needs to know it is truly her. Maybe this is a case of mistaken identity. Perhaps Marie told a friend her place was vacant since she had been staying with me and allowed her to seek shelter there. For a brief moment, I am filled with hope.

"Jax, even if I could let you see her, I would not. Her remains were taken to the mortuary in Shoreditch."

"But I could identify her. What if it is not her, Fred?"

"It's her. Joseph Barnett and John McCarthy officially identified her body. Barnett lived with her for many months and noted that he recognized her by her ear and her eyes. McCarthy was her landlord, and he confirmed Barnett's statement." He waves his hand. "You heard all this at the inquisition."

Marie talked about Barnett more out of fear. She was worried about his anger. I saw his anger the morning we paid him a visit, but I cannot deny he loved her as well. I have not met this McCarthy. I make a mental note to do so. "Have you questioned anyone other than those who testified yesterday?"

He nods. "Yes, we've spoken with several people who had seen her over the course of the night prior to her murder. Actually, more so than any of the other victims."

"Tell me."

He pulls another piece of paper from the file and hands it to me. "Here is the timeline of Kelly's movements the last several hours of her life. Some of this is a repetition from the inquisition; some is not."

I take the paper and read through it.

Thursday, November 8

7:30 pm – 8 pm, Barnett visits Kelly. He leaves at 8pm.

There are no confirmed sightings of Kelly between 8pm and 11:00pm

Sometime after 11pm and before 11:45pm Kelly was seen at the Britcanica drinking with a young man with a mustache. He appeared to be respectable and she appeared to be very drunk.

At 11:45 pm, Mary Cox, who lives at Miller's Court is returning home and sees Kelly accompanied by a stout man walking ahead of her. The man was carrying a pale of beer. She follows them, and they stop outside of Kelly's room. She passes them walking on to her room, says "good night." Kelly replies, "Good night, I am going to sing." Cox hears Kelly singing "A Violet from Mother's Grave" as she continues walking.

Kelly has a meal of fish and potatoes.

A note in the margin indicates that this determination comes from the autopsy report, which noted her last meal.

12:30 am, Catherine Pickett, a flower girl who lives near Kelly, is disturbed by her singing. She intends to complain, but her husband stops her.

1:00 am, Elizabeth Prater is waiting for a friend outside the entrance to Miller's Court. Prater lives directly above Mary Jane Kelly, number 20. She waits a half hour and then goes into McCarthy's to chat. She hears no singing and sees nobody. A few minutes pass, and she goes back to her room. She places two chairs in front of her door and goes to sleep. She states that she had too much to drink. Mrs. Cox goes out again.

> *3:00 am, Mrs. Cox returns home and notes there is no sound or light coming from Kelly's room. She states she occasionally hears comings and goings throughout the night but does not know what house.*
>
> *4:00 am, Elizabeth Prater is awakened by her cat. She hears a faint cry of "Oh, murder!" but thinks nothing of it, as the cry of murder is common in the district.*

Several other accounts are noted later in the morning hours, but they contradict the coroner's findings and estimated time of death. I hand the paper back to Fred. "Do you take stock in all these accounts?"

He takes the paper from me. "Some I do, but frankly, I think most of them just want their name in the papers."

I nod. "I tend to agree." I shift in the chair. "Do you mind if I talk to these people?"

"If I said yes, would you refrain?"

I laugh. "No."

"I thought so."

I chuckle as I rise from the chair. "You have been most helpful, Fred. I can't thank you enough for all you have given me."

"It's not my normal practice, but I believe there are extenuating circumstances here that warrants you knowing what we know. I agree with your theory of a connection to Marie and her past. I also agree the killer knows you as well." He gets up and walks toward me, then places his arm on my shoulder. "But I would not feel comfortable if I didn't give you a warning. The Ripper is cunning, and as you know, he's eluded capture through five murders, maybe more we don't know about or have not been able to link to him. Be careful and tread cautiously. Your life is at stake here, and I believe that if he knows you are closing in on him, he wouldn't think twice about coming after you or maybe even Victoria."

I nod, acknowledging his concerns. "I know, but I believe his ego will get the better of him when he does realize I am coming for him, and he will want me to catch him if only for the sake of bragging over what he has done and, more importantly, what he has gotten away with." I walk toward the door and open it. "I will be in touch."

I turn and walk out.

CHAPTER FOUR

Once outside, I contemplate all the information Fred gave me. So many people saw Marie the night of her murder, but I believe the best place to start is with the people I know. Stepping toward my carriage where Carlton is dutifully waiting for my return, I instruct, "Madame Grace's brothel, Carlton."

When we arrive, Carlton opens the door and I step out of the carriage. I turn back toward Carlton. "I'm going to be a while. Come back in an hour or so."

"But, sir?" Carlton never liked the Whitechapel district, and he certainly is not comfortable with me walking into a brothel. It is a good thing I'm the employer and he's the employee because in the coming weeks, I intend to spend a lot of time in this district and pubs and brothels.

"Carlton, go find some amusement," I say sarcastically.

Carlton scoffs, and I can't help the chuckle that escapes me as I walk to the door of the brothel. I walk inside and am immediately approached by a woman scantily dressed, which doesn't surprise me.

"What's your pleasure, sir?" she asks.

"I would like to see Madame Grace."

She pouts as she points at the stairs. "Top of the stairs, first door on the right."

"Thank you." I know exactly where I need to go and head straight for her office. I've been here before. When I get to her door, I knock. I hear shuffling in the room and footsteps approach.

The door opens, and I am surprised to see I am not greeted by Madame Grace but Joseph Barnett. Looking beyond him, I see Madame Grace sitting at her desk.

I take a good look at Barnett. When I saw him at Miller's Court last week, I never really looked at him. I was too busy being the victor of Marie's love. Looking at him now, he appears to be in his early thirties, medium built, and a bit shorter than me. He's also fair skinned—well, at least from what I can tell behind his bushy mustache and unshaven shadow on his face.

"Ahh, Mr. Kent," she calls. "I've been expecting you." She gets up from her chair and walks toward the door. "Funny that you both are here at the same time." She pushes her way past the man and comes directly to me, then pulls me into an embrace. Whispering, she says, "It's so awful about Marie."

I'm completely confused by the embrace as if we were old friends. Associates, yes. But friends?

"Do come in, Mr. Kent."

Barnett steps aside a little more, and I walk in. As I step past him, the smell of fish fills the air. *Marie's last meal was fish and potatoes.* I immediately turn back to him and eye him warily.

"I assume you are here for the same reason as Mr. Barnett?" Madame Grace asks.

Still eyeing Barnett, I cannot help but think about all the grief this man caused Marie. At times, I felt she was afraid of him and his wrath as she hinted how he could be abusive. *Is he the killer and just putting on a good act? Did he kill her because she did not want him? Did he kill her because she wanted me?*

I take in his appearance and quickly convince myself there is no way he could be the Ripper. He's nothing but a man who has a broken heart. We both have lost Maria. He wants answers, and maybe, just maybe, we can put our jealousies aside and work together on this and find some justice for our beloved Marie. It is time for the two of us to work together.

Madame Grace breaks the silence again. "Mr. Kent, please meet Mr. Barnett."

I hold out my hand in an attempt to be civil. "We met a few days ago." Still holding my hand out for him to shake, I say, "Although I do not believe we were formally introduced."

Barnett is hesitant at first and grumbles, but then reluctantly he holds out his hand and shakes mine. "Eh, good to meet you."

"I was just about to tell Mr. Barnett what I knew about your beloved Marie."

We both turn back toward Madame Grace eagerly. "Please sit down, gentlemen." We both sit in the two chairs opposite her desk and patiently wait for her to begin speaking.

"I saw Marie the night of her death. She came by here looking for work. She seemed a bit agitated when I told her all the work had been divided out for the evening."

I interrupt. "She was afraid for her life."

They both look at me in astonishment.

"Perhaps I should explain. When Marie left my home at St. James Place on the late afternoon of November 8, she left in fear because she believed I was the Ripper."

Madame Grace gasps. "Mr. Kent!" she exclaims as she stands.

I motion with my hand for her to sit. "I am not the Ripper."

Barnett chimes in. "And we're just supposed to believe you?"

"Yes." I remain calm, but Barnett does not.

He rises from his chair and comes at me, fists cocked and ready.

I hold out my hand to stop him. "Before you shoot off that hot temper of yours, will you just listen?"

Barnett stops advancing toward me.

"I believe the Ripper is someone from Marie's past. She knew him. And more importantly, I believe I have come in contact with him at some point, but I don't know when."

Barnett sits back down.

I look over at him. "I believe he used me and my sister..." I look at Madame Grace, and she nods. "To get to Marie."

I wait for them to say something or a reaction, but I get nothing.

"I'm going to track him down."

Barnett scoffs. "What makes you think you can catch him when the police can't?"

"Because, Mr. Barnett, he wants me to catch him. He wants to brag and tell me his whole story." I lean back in my chair. "Think about this. The three of us have spent more time with Marie in the last few months than anyone else. All three of us were close to her. I believe we can pool our resources, tell what we know, and perhaps it will bring us one step closer to catching a killer." I wait. "Agreed?"

"Agreed," says Madame Grace, and Barnett just nods. I guess it's an agreement.

Just then, there is a light knock on the door.

"Come in," Madame Grace says.

The door opens slowly, and a small girl walks in. She appears to be five or six years of age with adorable blonde curls. She wears a loose, probably-too-big smock-type dress, her face is dirty, and she is barefoot, her feet just as dirty as her face.

"Ah, Ginny."

"Forgive me for intruding, Madame," she says in a sweet yet frail voice. "Lucette took Mrs. Conner and won't give her back."

Madame laughs. "Well, we can't let Lucette have Mrs. Conner, now can we?"

The child shakes her head. "No. Mrs. Conner is *my* dolly."

Madame Grace gets up from her desk. "Excuse me, gentlemen, I shall return. I have to save Mrs. Conner." She makes her way to the door, the child following close behind her.

The awkwardness between Barnett and me, who are now alone in Madame Grace's office, does not escape my notice. The tension is thick and uncomfortable. Neither of us speaks to the other, and as much as it might help to ease things between us, we remain quiet.

A few minutes later, Madame Grace returns alone. "So sorry about the intrusion." She rushes into the room toward her desk. "The poor child has nobody but me and the girls who live here."

"She doesn't—"

"Oh gawd no!"

Relief washes over me. For a minute, I was worried the child was doing what the rest of the girls did in this house. "She's the daughter of one of my girls. I guess you could say I've raised her since she was three."

"How old is she?" I'm not sure why curiosity strikes me with regard to this child. Perhaps it's because I am totally surprised to see a child in a place like this. I never thought about the consequences these women face in the in the line of work they chose. I guess you could call getting pregnant an occupational hazard. This thought makes me very sad as I think about how many unwanted children are out there because of this.

I shake these melancholy thoughts from my mind when Madame Grace speaks. "She's six. She's lived here three years."

Barnett fidgets in his seat. He's impatient. Marie was right; he has a short fuse. *What did she ever see in this guy?* I think to myself. And then, the answer strikes me: a meal ticket. *Did she think the same about me?* This thought saddens me, and the more I think about it, she had. At first. Neither of us planned to fall in love. I needed comfort, and she needed money. It was a win-win for both of us. But as the weeks passed, we both knew we had found our true mate. Well, until she thought I was a murderer.

"Madame Grace, if you need anything for the child, please contact me."

"That's very generous of you, Mr. Kent, considering..." Her voice trails off.

"Considering?"

She shakes her head. "Oh, don't mind me. My mind tends to scatter at times. I meant nothing of it."

"Very well. So, Madame Grace, I assume you have known Marie the longest. Why don't you start by telling me what you know about her? What brought her here? Is there any back history that you think might help us here?"

She sits back in her chair. "I can only convey what she has told me, Mr. Kent. She was a known storyteller, so I cannot attest to validity of her story."

"Understood."

"She was born in Limerick. She was from a well-to-do family. When she was sixteen, she married a collier and moved to Wales. This displeased her family, and they pretty much disowned her. Three years after she was married, her husband was killed in a mine explosion. She spent the next couple of years doing odd jobs to earn a living. She scrubbed floors, washed other people's laundry, and even sold flowers on the street. She also had told me that during this time, she spent a lot of time ill." She stands from her chair and begins to pace.

"She arrived in London around 1884. She was twenty-one. I met her around April, when she arrived in the East End." She sits on the corner of her desk.

"So you don't know what happened to her between her arrival in London and when you met her?"

"No. Every time I asked her about it, she would brush it off with something funny or ignore it all together."

Barnett speaks up. "I do."

We both look at him, eager to hear what he has to say.

"I met Marie around March or April of this year. She had just returned from Paris and was looking in the East End for work. When I commented that a woman as beautiful as she need not look in this district, for she belonged in the West End, she laughed and said she never wanted to go back there again." He looks at me and gives me what I think to be a glare.

Is he angry with me because I took her back to the west side? Maybe because he could not?

"We hit it off straight away, and within a couple of weeks, she had found work with the Madame and had moved in with me at Miller's Court. We had been living together ever since, until you came along." He glances at me and glares again.

He does blame me for all of this. "I understand from the police that you moved out a few days ago."

"I did. We had an argument. It was bad, and my temper got the best of me." He stops, and I look at him encouragingly. He shrugs. "Yeah, we argued about you. I wanted her to quit hooking and marry me. She would not leave you. She said she loved you. That's when I exploded and stormed out. It was the last time I saw her alive."

I can't help the smile that comes across my face. I hate the thought of him being angry with Marie, but I have to say it is comforting to hear him say she did love me. "If it is any consolation to you, I loved her too."

"Well that makes both of us," Barnett says sadly. He looks down and fidgets with his hands. "Anyway, the last time I saw her alive was at half past seven the night before she died."

"At 13 Miller's Court?" I remembered that from his testimony yesterday.

"Yes. I had heard she was back in Whitechapel and thought perhaps she had changed her mind and left you. I doubted it, but I couldn't let the chance pass by without looking into it first." He takes a deep breath. "And honestly I was worried about her and wanted to check up on her and make sure she was okay." Leaning over in his chair, he puts his head in his hands. "She was extremely agitated and quick to have me leave. She had been drinking, and I could tell she was scared. When I had tried to console her, she begged me to leave. She kept saying *'He will be coming for me. You must not be here when he does.'* He lifts his head up. "I assumed she meant you." Tears welled in his eyes. "If I had known she was talking about the Ripper, I would have never left her alone." He leans back in his chair. "And you wanna know what the real stick of it all is? She had told me she had left you but that she had not changed her mind about me." He wipes his eyes. "She didn't even want me after you were out of the picture."

I could not help but feel for him. He really did love her, and I can empathize with that. "Did she ever tell you anything about her trip to Paris or her time in the West End?"

He nods. "She took a job in an upscale brothel, and there was a man there who took a liking to Marie. She told me his name was Carlisle Hamilton, and she lived with him for some time. He was the man who took her to Paris."

"What broke the relationship up?"

"She said he was very possessive. He wanted her to stop doing tricks, and she refused." He shakes his head. "I know exactly how Hamilton felt. I begged her to quit for months."

"Do you know anything about this Carlisle Hamilton?"

He shakes his head again. "Just that he is wealthy and lives in the West End." He waits and then says, "I'd think you would know more about him than I. After all, isn't that where you live?"

I nod. I think about the name Carlisle Hamilton. It sounds so familiar, but it is also a common British name. There are probably millions of Carlisle Hamiltons in England. "I knew about the trip to Paris. She mentioned it in passing as one of the worst experiences of her life. She said the man who had accompanied her was a sadist and was twisted to the point that many times she thought he was going to kill her. She never said how she got away from him. Do you know?"

"Every night she stole money from him. She knew where he kept his extra funds hidden, and when he slept, she would take a little and add it to her secret stash. She was smart enough to only take a little at a time to ensure nothing was missed. When she stole enough to pay for passage back to England, she left during the night while he was asleep. From what she told me, she never saw him again, but there were numerous times when I felt she was looking over her shoulder."

I think about what Barnett has told me. Carlisle Hamilton is well off and lived in the West End. His name is so familiar. I shall plan a night at White's. White's is a prestigious gentlemen's club.

Its exclusivity is not all about how much money you pay but, more importantly to them, who you are and who you know.

"Madame Grace, do you know anything about this Carlisle Hamilton?"

She looks at me nervously, glancing at the door to her office and then back at me. Then, as relaxed as cat, she says, "Mr. Barnett has pretty much covered all I know about him. Marie did talk about him, not so much about her relationship with the man but more worried that he should come after her. I always felt she was looking over her shoulder, afraid her past would come back to haunt her."

I stand, reach into my pocket, and pull out two of my calling cards. "You both have been very helpful. If you think of anything further, you can call on me anytime."

"Mr. Kent, you are not worried about..." She looks at Barnett and then back at me. "Our kind calling on you?"

"Madame Grace, I would hope that after all this time and my relationship with Marie and my sister, whom I assume is still in your care, you would know none of that social class hypocrisy means anything to me. If you and Mr. Barnett have some information you think will help, you are welcome at my home any time." I walk toward the door but turn back. "I'm going to catch him. You can be sure of that. I believe we all want that."

They both nod and I turn back toward the door, open it, and walk out.

As I make my way downstairs to the main door, I pass Ginny carrying a tray of tea into one of the rooms. *This is no place for a child.* The thought of a young child serving prostitutes really bothers me. No child deserves this kind of life. *Where is her mother?*

I step outside. I pull my scarf snug around my neck to block the chill in the air and make my way to my carriage. "Let's go home, Carlton."

"Indeed, sir." Carlton opens the door, and I step inside. He readies the horses and we're off. I spend the entire trip in deep thought about all I heard today. And then, before I know it, I find myself thinking about Ginny.

Oh, my dear Mr. Kent. Do you really believe I am not aware of your plans? Do you really believe I have not orchestrated things in this way? Next to Marie, you are my worst enemy. Do you know why? I live for the moment when I can tell you.

CHAPTER FIVE

The next day, I spend most of my time in my study reviewing my notes and organizing my thoughts on the case. After several hours of being sequestered, there is a knock at the door. "Come in."

Rothschild steps inside and says, "Forgive the intrusion, sir, but you have a visitor."

"Who?" I very rarely get visitors, so it escapes my mind as to whom this visitor could be.

"A Joseph Barnett, sir, and a George Hutchinson."

Yes, I forgot I gave Barnett and Madame Grace my calling card. Eagerly, I rise from my chair. He could have important information.

"Please send them both in." A few minutes later, Barnett and another gentleman I assume is George Hutchinson enters my study.

Barnett is looking around in awe. "You sure do have a nice place here, Mr. Kent."

"Thank you. And it's Jax."

"Uh, yeah, Jax." He points at the man next to him and says, "This here is George Hutchinson."

I look at him curiously.

"He saw Marie for some time Friday morning. I thought you might want to hear what he has to say."

"Indeed, I do." I gesture toward the chairs in the room. "Gentlemen, please make yourself comfortable. Sit." Once they are seated, I walk to the sitting area and sit down myself. "So, Mr.

Hutchinson, Barnett seems to think you have some information I might find useful. I'm listening."

"Well..." He looks at Barnett who nods and encourages him to go on. "I have known Marie for about a year now. I've uh," he stumbles, "used her services in the past on a couple of occasions." He waits for a reaction, and when he gets nothing, he seems to relax and continues. "I had not seen Marie walking the streets for many nights before the morning of the ninth, and I honestly thought something had happened to her. I may have not been with her every night, but I always saw her. But for the last couple of months, there wasn't any sign of her. Then on the morning of the ninth, I saw her. It was around two, and I was walking down Thrawl Street. A man in a long dark cloak rushed past me, but I paid him no mind. I assumed he was in a hurry." He fidgets in his seat.

"When I reached the intersection at Flower and Dean, I ran into Marie. I could tell she had been drinking. She asked me for some sixpence. I told her I had none and her response was 'I must go and find some money.'" He shrugs his shoulders. "It's not uncommon for the prostitutes of Whitechapel to walk the streets looking for money. If they did not get a john for the night, they had to make money somehow. But it was odd because Marie never asked for money unless she was working, if you get my meaning."

Barnett and I both sigh at the same time. Unfortunately, we both get his meaning, but even though we knew what Marie was, it doesn't mean we liked it.

"She turned to leave and walked in the direction of Thrawl Street where I had just came from. Again, it was odd for her to ask for money and I thought perhaps she might be in trouble, so I followed her." He rakes his hands through his hair. "I kept a good distance behind her until I saw her meet up with the man I had passed earlier. I watched closely as the man put his hand on her shoulder and, leaning in, he whispered in her ear. Marie laughed and replied, 'All right.' Then I heard the man say, 'You will be all right for what I have told you,' which I have to say made no sense to me." He leans forward in his chair. "The man placed his arm around Marie's shoulder, and they walked together like that down Commercial Street toward Dorset Street." He pauses and closes his eyes. He must be trying to recreate the scene as he tells his story. "It was his right arm that was around Marie's shoulders. In the left he carried a parcel or bag of some sort."

"Do you believe, Mr. Hutchinson, that you may have seen the killer?" I wanted him to finish, but I just had to interrupt and ask.

"Sir, I believe I have."

"And why didn't you come forward for the inquisition if you believed this?"

He hesitates and then says, "I kept thinking it through over and over. I just wanted to make sure I had everything accurate. When I believed I had, that's when I went to find Joe. I knew he and Marie were close, and well, sir, I didn't want the police to think I was looking for fame or something."

I nod. "Go on with your story, Mr. Hutchinson."

"So, I continued to follow them as they walked to the Queen's Head Public House. While standing under a street light in front of that establishment, I was able to get a look at the man."

"And?" I prod.

"He was pale with a slight mustache turned up at the corners. His hair was dark. He was wearing a soft felt hat pulled down over his eyes, a long dark coat trimmed in astrakhan collar and cuffs, dark trousers, and a white collar with a black necktie fixed with a horseshoe pin. There was a massive gold chain in his waistcoat with a large seal. A red stone was hanging from it. He carried kid gloves in one hand and, like I said, a small package or parcel in the other. I would guess him to be five six or five seven, and I would estimate is he's around thirty-five or thirty-six years old."

"If I got an artist in here, would you repeat that description for him?"

He nods. "Of course, anything I can do to help catch this monster."

"Good. Anything else?"

"Yes, Marie and the man did not enter the Queens Head Pub but crossed Commercial Street and continue down Dorset Street. As they passed me, the man put down his head as if to hide his eyes. I watch as they stop outside Miller's Court and talk for quite some time. I heard Marie say, 'All right, my dear. Come along, and you'll be comfortable.' The man placed his arm on her shoulder and gave her a kiss. She then said, 'I seemed to have lost my handkerchief.' The man pulled out a red one and gave it to her. They stood there for another minute or so and then proceeded down Miller's Court toward Marie's room. I then walked forward and waited at the entrance. I could not see them anymore, but something told me to wait to see if they came out. So I did."

"Did they come back out?"

"No, I waited for about forty-five minutes. Nobody came out, and I left." He hesitates for a second and then says, "I did recognize someone who went down Miller's Court after Marie and the man had."

"Who? Was it a man?" I was anxious. Maybe the man wasn't the killer, but this other person was.

"No, a laundress, Sarah Lewis. I know her husband pretty well and have seen her around Miller's Court quite a bit. I believe her parents live there." He turns and looks at Barnett. "But unless she had some difficulties with her husband, it is not normal for her to be out that late, or early in the morning." He scoffs. "I guess it's all semantics when you think about it."

I eye him curiously. Where did that come from? "Mr. Hutchinson, I'm not sure I understand your meaning."

He waves his hand. "Of course you do. When you are talking about three o'clock in the morning, some refer to it as late at night and others refer to it as the wee hours of morning. But really, it's all semantics."

I'm not sure I buy his response, but I will let it go for now. I look him over. Could this man be the killer? I think about his description of the man with Marie. He said the man was fair and had dark hair and a mustache that was curled at the ends. Now that

I look closely, he has described himself. Could this man have come forward to guarantee he would not be considered a suspect? I wonder...

I stand. "Do you have anything more to tell us?"

Hutchinson stands and shakes his head. "No, I believe I have told you everything."

I look at him. I am roughly six feet and one inch. I walk toward Hutchinson and gauge his height against my own. He's about three to four inches shorter than me. He's about five feet nine inches. This is just too coincidental.

I hold my hand out to shake it. He takes my hand, and I look into his eyes and say, "Thank you for coming forward. I'm sure you have given us some very helpful information."

"It was my pleasure, sir."

I look for the recognition I had hoped I would find in his eyes. I don't see it, but that will not discount my suspicions of this man.

I turn toward Barnett. "Thank you for bringing him here."

Barnett nods and gets up.

As the two gentlemen prepare to leave, I say, "Mr. Hutchinson, I expect you will take your story to Inspector Abberline?"

"Well, I... I was not planning to."

"And why is that?" I step closer to him.

He's nervous now and fidgets. "I thought you would tell my story."

"Ah, Mr. Hutchinson. It does not work that way. You know better than that. So, let me rephrase. You will take your story to Inspector Abberline. Correct?"

He doesn't answer, so I step even closer and look him directly in the eye.

"Because if you do not in the next twenty-four hours, I will."

He looks relieved.

"I will, and I will make sure you are added to the inspector's suspect list."

"But... but... I am not the Ripper!"

"Perhaps not, but perhaps you are. I really do not know, but the fact that you did not go directly to the police with your story tells me I need to be cautious with you." I brush a piece of lint off his shoulder. "Tell your story to the inspector, Mr. Hutchinson, and clear your name. You wouldn't want any unnecessary inquiries into you or your family, now would you?"

He shakes his head. "No, sir, I wouldn't." He turns toward Barnett. "I guess we are going to H Division next."

Barnett grins and nods.

I follow both gentlemen out of the study and into the foyer. "Rothschild, please have Carlton prepare the carriage. These gentlemen are going to H Division in Whitechapel. I'd like him to take them."

"Will you be going with them, sir?"

"No, I have things to tend to in town. When Carlton returns, I should be ready to leave. Please inform him I will need his services when he returns."

"Very well, sir." Rothschild leaves and returns in less than five minutes. He hands the men their wraps. They both thank me again and leave.

Once they have left the foyer, I make my way upstairs. Carlton will be back in a couple of hours.

CHAPTER SIX

Carlton and I make our way to Whitechapel. I want to go to H Division and speak with Fred to ensure Barnett and Hutchinson did indeed stop to see him. And, I have to say, I am curious to know if the story Hutchinson told me was the same he told Abberline.

"Jax, good to see you again!" Fred exclaims as I walk into his office.

"Fred, hello." I take a seat. "So tell me, did you receive a visit today from Joe Barnett and George Hutchinson?"

"I did. They told me they went to see you first and that you sent them to me."

I nod.

"Interesting story Hutchinson has."

"Indeed." I lean back in the chair and cross my leg over my opposite knee. "What did Hutchinson tell you?"

Fred proceeds to tell me what Hutchinson said, and I am surprised to say there are only a few discrepancies— minor ones at that. I know when a story is repeated several times it risks changing, and I was worried perhaps he would have said something entirely different.

When he finished, he stated, "Our stenographer is typing his statement up as we speak."

"Good, may I get a copy?"

He nods. "Of course." He leans forward in his chair. "What do you make of this Sarah Lewis?"

"You know, I was thinking about that after he left. She seemed so insignificant when Hutchinson mentioned her, but the more I thought about it, I realized she walked right down Miller's Court. If something were happening, sounds or even light coming from Marie's room, she would have seen it."

"I thought the same. Hutchinson said her friend lives at two Miller's Court. Did you hear her testimony at the inquisition?"

"I don't remember her, and I have not had a chance to read the transcripts you gave me."

"Read it. I believe she may know more than she is telling us. Might be something worth looking into. I think she may be more forthcoming talking to you instead of the police."

"I will."

"So, have you found out anything new since we last spoke?"

I hesitate at first, not sure I want him to know everything I know, but then I quickly realize we are on the same team. As much as I want to be the one to catch him, providing all the information I have to Fred can only help. "I talked at length the other day with Madame Grace and Joe Barnett. There is a questionable character in Marie's past I need to look into."

"Really? Do you know his name?"

"Yes, Carlisle Hamilton, but I'm sure this is an alias. I think he may be a gentleman in London Society and is protecting himself with a different name."

He shakes his head. "I do not recognize the name, but you know more society men than I do. Do you?"

"No, which is why I think it is an alias, but I have a feeling I know him. Like I told you the other day, this is personal."

"I agree, it is personal." He pauses for a moment, and then says, "So what is next?"

"I will be making some inquiries with the House of Lords members. Since I am a member, it provides me an in, and frankly, it is a good place to start."

He nods.

"Well, I don't want to take up any more of your time. I merely came by to check up on Hutchinson." I get up from the chair. "I do not know about him. There is something I do not trust."

"I thought the same thing."

I turn to leave. When I get to the door, I turn back. "Thank you for seeing me. Let's keep the lines of communication open."

"Agreed. Have a good afternoon, Jax."

I turn the knob and walk out.

Fred has me thinking about Sarah Lewis now, so instead of going to the House of Lords like I had planned, I decided to have Carlton take me back home. I hate that I cannot remember her testimony and need to go back and read it.

***

Once I arrive home, I hole myself up in my study and pull out the transcript Fred gave me the other day. As I'm shuffling through the pages, I finally come to Ms. Lewis's testimony.

> *"I live at 24 Great Powell Street, Spitalfields. I am a laundress. I know Mrs. Keyler in Miller's Court. I was at her house at half past 2 on Friday morning. She lives at No.2 in the court on the left on the first floor. I know the time by having looked at the Spitalfields Church clock as I passed it before I entered the court.*
>
> *When I went in the court, I saw a man opposite the court on Dorset Street standing alone by the lodging house. He was not tall but stout and had on a black wide-awake hat. I did not notice his clothes. Another young man with a woman passed by. The man was still standing in the street and was looking up the court as if waiting for someone to come out."*

I think about this. She is talking about George Hutchinson, and she describes him perfectly. He stated he had waited outside the Court on Dorset Street. I continue to read.

> *"I went to Mrs. Keyler's. I was awake all night in a chair, and I heard no noise. Then I dozed off, and I woke up about half past three. I sat awake until nearly five. A little before four, I heard a female voice shout loudly, "Oh, murder!" The sound seemed to come from the direction of the deceased's room, but there was only one scream."*

Of course there was only one scream. If he slit her throat first as we believe, she would not have been able to utter another sound afterward. I continue.

> *"I took no notice of it. I left Mrs. Keyler's at about half past 5 the afternoon of 9 November, as the police would not let us out before.*

Fred did not tell me he had detained witnesses all afternoon. Did he spend all that time questioning them, or did he have them wait for no apparent reason? Of course he had a reason, silly of me to think otherwise. I continue with Sarah Lewis's testimony.

> *"About Wednesday night prior at 8 o'clock, I was going along Bethnal Green Road with another female when a gentleman passed us. He then turned back and asked us to follow him. He said he did not mind if one of us refused. Then he took a couple of steps away and came back. He said if we would follow him, he would treat us. He asked us to go down a passage. He had a bag and put it down asking us, 'What are you frightened of?' He then began to undo his coat and felt for something. We got scared and ran away. I remember him clearly.*

He was short, pale faced with a black mustache. The bag he carried was about nine inches to a foot long. He wore a round high hat and a brownish long overcoat with a short black coat underneath. He wore pepper and salt trousers. I would guess he was about forty years of age.

"On our running away, we did not look after the man. Then, on the Friday morning of the murder, about half past two when I was coming to Miller's Court, I met the same man with a female in Commercial Street near Mr. Ringer's Public House, near the market. He had then no overcoat on, but he had the bag and the same hat, trousers, and undercoat.

"I passed by them and looked back at the man. I was frightened. I looked back again when I got to the corner of Dorset Street. I worried for the woman he was with. I have not seen the man since, but I should know him if I did."

Could this woman possibly be the one person who can identify the Ripper? I think for a moment. If indeed the man she saw was the man with Marie and if he was the killer... Or did he leave and another man approach 13 Miller's Court? I drop the paper from my hands and slam them on the desk. "Damn!" I shout out loud. The uncertainty of all this is tearing me up inside. So many fucking unanswered questions. I lie my head on my desk and close my eyes. I'm too tired and frustrated to make my way to my bedchamber. Perhaps in sleep I will find answers in my dreams.

CHAPTER SEVEN

The next morning, I am awakened by Rothschild. I'm still in my study, and I awake with a huge crick in my neck, as I am still at my desk.

"Sir, are you unwell?" Rothschild asks.

"Yes, Rothschild. Last night I was going over notes on the case and laid my head down for a brief rest. I guess I was more tired than I thought." I smirk.

"If you do not mind me saying, sir, you are emotionally exhausted on top of being physically tired. Miss Marie's death has taken its toll on you."

I get up from the desk and stretch. "I know. You are right, but I'm in this now. I cannot stop."

"Oh, sir, you misunderstand. I am not suggesting you stop, just that you take care of yourself. Take some time to grieve, sir. It will help."

I shake my head. "That, Rothschild, I cannot do. I will not be able to properly grieve for Marie until her killer is in jail or, preferably, dead."

He has no retort to my last comment and quickly changes the subject. "Well, what do we have planned today?"

"Well, actually, I think the police may have a break in the case. The gentleman who came over here yesterday talked about a man. Another witness, Sarah Lewis, confirms and testified at the inquisition of seeing this man as well. I believe they both have seen the Ripper." I walk back to my desk to look at my notes and the papers scattered there. "Or, the gentleman from yesterday is the killer because he matches the description they both gave." I look back up at Rothschild and shrug. "Although it can be possible, I find it highly unlikely. I really think the Ripper is an upper-class gentleman hiding behind his name and riches."

I walk around the desk. "So with all that being said, I would like you to have a bath drawn for me and tell Carlton to be ready with the carriage in about an hour."

Rothschild nods and turns to leave. I grab my waistcoat that was lying on the couch and follow him out.

An hour later, I am sitting in my carriage, and Carlton and I are heading to Whitechapel. Never in a million years did I think I would be spending so much time in the East End that did not involve Victoria. *Victoria.* Madame Grace said she was doing well, but I wonder. I have not received any word on the contrary, so I am going to go with no news is good news.

My plan for the day is to find Ms. Lewis, and I need to speak with Mr. and Mrs. McCarthy, Marie's landlords. I really want to see the place where the murder took place, but I doubt they will let me near her room. Regardless, I intend to ask.

Sarah Lewis testified that she lived at 24 Great Powell Street, Spitalfields, so as we pull up to the address stated, I assume the woman out front is Mrs. Lewis.

Stepping out of the carriage, I say, "Hello."

She hurries along toward the door.

"Please, Mrs. Lewis?" I ask.

She turns her head back toward me, her hand eagerly on the doorknob. "Who wants to know?"

I take a step toward her. "My name is Jackson Kent, and I was engaged to Mary Kelly."

She relaxes her hand on the knob and completely turns to face me.

"Go on, Mary Kelly was not engaged!" she exclaims.

I reach for her arm. "Actually, she was." I hesitate and then say, "If you will just give me a few minutes of your time, I can explain everything."

She looks around worried.

"Mrs. Lewis, it is daylight and we can stand right here out in the open in front of your home."

She nods and steps away from the door.

"Like I said, my name is Jackson Kent." I proceed with my story, and by the time I am done, she is sitting on her front stoop in tears.

"Oh, Mr. Kent, I am so sorry for your loss. You know, I testified in her inquisition. I believe I may have seen the Ripper."

I sit down next to her. "Thank you. And yes, that is why I am here. I have been working with Inspector Abberline on the case and was reading over your testimony last night. And, I agree with you. I think you may have seen the Ripper as well."

She smiles.

"So tell me, Mrs. Lewis, do you know a George Hutchinson?"

She looks at me quizzically. "I do."

"We have received testimony from him, and he basically collaborates your testimony, but there is one thing that just doesn't check out."

"And that is, Mr. Kent?"

"Well, in your testimony, you indicate you saw a man and woman walking down Miller's Court and you saw a man standing outside the court as if waiting for someone."

She nods. "That is correct."

"Well, what I was wondering was could they be the same man?"

She pauses before she answers, and it looks like she is replaying the scene in her mind. After cocking her head a few times as if to question herself, she finally speaks. "I don't think so, Mr. Kent. My memory is clear. They were two different men."

"Well then, that answers my question." I stand from the stoop. "Is there anything else you can think of? Perhaps something that came to mind after your testimony that you think may be helpful?"

She shakes her head. "I believe I told the police everything I could remember."

I nod. "Very well then." I reach in my pocket and pull out one of my calling cards. "If you think of anything, no matter how small or insignificant you may think it is, please do not hesitate to call on me." I hand her the card, and she takes it. "Thank you, Mrs. Lewis, for your time. I apologize if I scared you at first. I honestly did not think how a total stranger approaching you might scare you, especially with a killer on the loose. Forgive me."

She waves her hands. "Think nothing of it, Mr. Kent." She turns to go into the house as I head for the carriage. "Mr. Kent?" she calls back at me.

I turn back to face her.

"I am very sorry for your loss," she says sadly, turns back to her door, and enters the house.

I make my way to my carriage and step inside. Carlton approaches the window. "Where to, sir?"

"Miller's Court, Dorset Street." He frowns and then proceeds to his post, and we are off. When we head down Commercial Street toward Dorset, the thought of actually seeing the murder scene makes my stomach turn. I'm sure the blood will still be there and will have started to stain. The smell will be gruesome. However, Marie will be gone, for her body had been taken to the mortuary in Shoreditch days ago. To my knowledge, she has not been laid to rest yet. *I wonder why?*

We turn down Dorsett Street, which is the heart of the area's rookery. It's a slum, unfortunately occupied by the very poor, prostitutes and criminals. The area is overcrowded, low-quality housing with little to no sanitation, so it's not only the fact of where I am, but the smell adds to the nausea I am feeling.

Carlton pulls the carriage up and comes around to open my door. I definitely stand out. I never thought much about her living in these conditions before when Marie and I visited here. Perhaps it did not bother me then because I knew I was taking her away to a better life. I think back to that day. I was her hero. *Some hero I turned out to be.*

As I walk down the alleyway toward Miller's Court, my heart grows heavy. My legs feel like dead weights, and it takes immense effort to take each step. To sway my mind in another direction, I look around at the poorly constructed buildings. The area is cramped, and it is clear it is densely populated. Until I came along, this was her life.

I pass a woman in the alley. "Excuse me," I say.

The lady stops and hesitates.

"Can you tell me where I can find Jack McCarthy?"

She points in the opposite direction. "That way, right next door. This is number twenty-six Dorset. His chandler's shop is number twenty-seven Dorset Street."

I tip my hat. "Thank you. Good day."

She continues to walk as I watch her go. If I go the way she said, then I go away from Marie's room. *Perhaps I should just stumble upon it before I see Mr. McCarthy?* I turn back the way I was heading and head straight for number thirteen. It just occurs to me the taboo of the number thirteen. Why did I not think of it before?

As I approach her room, I walk slower. *Oh God, why am I doing this?* I question. In my head, God replies, *Because you need to know. You need to see it to ensure her death is real.* And that is the truth. I need something to confirm this nightmare indeed happened.

I spot number thirteen and notice as I approach that there is no door. Then I remember Fred had the door broken down so they could get inside. I glance at the window with the broken glass; I still do not understand why they did not just enter that way. I shake my head in confusion and step inside. There are bloodstains on the walls, floor, bed, and nightstand. Memories of the autopsy report fill my head.

> *The body was lying naked in the middle of the bed, the shoulders flat but the axis of the body inclined to the left side of the bed.*
>
> *The right arm was slightly abducted from the body and rested on the mattress.*
>
> *The tissues of the neck were severed all round down to the bone.*
>
> *The face was gashed in all directions, the nose, cheeks...*

I cannot take any more and turn to leave. I stop in the doorway and just stand there, my back to the murder scene. Closing my eyes, I take a deep breath. The sulfur smell of blood fills my nostrils.

I wait. And then I feel it.

I feel her.

She is here.

"Oh God, Marie, I love you," I whisper aloud. And although I cannot hear her or see her, I know she is standing here with me and heard me.

Her words fill my head. *"I'm so sorry, Jax. The fairy tale is over."* Her final words were for me.

"Marie," I whisper with an exasperated breath. She is right. The fairytale is over. "But know this, my love: I will avenge your death. I may die in the process, which only means I will see you sooner, but I assure you he will die too." I step out of the room and walk down the alleyway back toward Dorset Street. Tears stream down my face. She is really gone. I wipe the tears and walk on.

Rushing past me as I leave Miller's Court is a young girl. I look again and realize it is Ginny from Madame Grace's. "Ginny!" I call.

She stops and turns. "Sir?"

"Do you remember me?"

She smiles. "I do. You were visiting Madame."

I nod. "Yes, I was." I take a step toward her. "What are you doing here?"

"Madame sent me down here to retrieve something from Marie's room."

"What is that?" I ask curiously.

"A shawl. Madame said she gave it to her as a present and wants it back." What is that woman thinking sending a child down here and into Marie's room? I have said it before, and I will say it again. The brothel is no place for a child. I need to speak with Madame Grace about that.

"Ginny, why do you not let me go in Marie's room and get the scarf for you. It really is not a place for a little girl."

She smiles and sighs in relief. "Oh, thank you, sir. I was so afraid to go in there. I know Marie died in there."

I give her a hug. She is such a sweet thing. "What does the shawl look like? Do you know?"

She nods. "Madame says it is red." Well then, I turn back toward Marie's room and realize I have to go back in there. But Ginny should not be going in there either. Walking toward the door, I take a deep breath, then walk in. I realize for the first time Marie did not have many possessions. I look around the room and notice that besides the bed and the nightstand table, there is a fireplace and next to it a cabinet. Perhaps the shawl is in there. There are no other possessions lying around, and I'm afraid the police may have removed everything as evidence.

I walk to the cabinet and open it. I rummage through the few things inside, but to my disappointment, there is no red shawl. I stand and scan the room. There, in the middle of the room is another table I did not notice before. I was focused on the bed where the murder had occurred. Draped over a chair at the table is a red shawl. I walk over and take it in my hands. Holding it up to my nose, I can smell the sweet lavender perfume Marie used to wear when she lived with me.

"Oh, Marie, none but the lonely hearts can know my sadness," I whisper aloud.

And then, just as before, I feel her presence again. *"Love lives forever, Jax."* A small tear rolls down my cheek, and I think to myself as I walk toward the doorway, *Yes, my love, it does.* Wiping the tear away, I step outside, and Ginny is nervously waiting for me.

"Here you go, luv," I say to her, handing her the shawl.

"Oh!" she squeals. "Thank you so very much. Madame will be pleased."

She turns to leave, but I stop her and say, "You should not be walking around here alone." I walk her out of the entrance to Miller's Court and point at Carlton and my carriage. "Why don't you wait in there for me. I shall be a few more minutes, and I will take you back to Madame Grace."

"Oh, sir, I could not! Madame will be angry."

"I know Madame very well. I will deal with her. Now go wait in the carriage for me." I walk her over and open the door. She gets inside, and I turn toward Carlton. "Keep her here until I return."

He nods.

"I shall not be long." I head back and make my way to McCarthy's.

CHAPTER EIGHT

Stepping inside McCarthy's shop, I look around for Mr. McCarthy. There is a man at the counter, and I approach. "Excuse me, I am looking for John McCarthy?" I ask.

"Who's lookin' for 'im?"

I pull out my calling card. "My name is Jackson Kent, and I was a friend of Miss Kelly who lived across the way." He takes my card and looks at it. I wonder if the man can read as he glances at it quickly and flips it over and then back again. He steps away from the counter and goes in the back without saying a word.

A few seconds later, a tall slender man comes forward. "You looking for me?" he asks as he steps up to the counter.

"Are you John McCarthy?"

"Yes, I am." He looks over the clerk again and then says, "And this is Thomas Bowyer."

Oh, this is the man who discovered her body.

I smile at them. "May I ask you both some questions?"

"I do not know. I mean I know your name, but who are you now?" McCarthy asks.

"Forgive me, as you know, my name is Jackson Kent. I am the man whom Miss Kelly has been staying with the last couple of months, prior to her death."

Bowyer gasps, and McCarthy looks at me warily. "Well, Barnett did say she was stomping with some wealthy man in St. James Park." He looks down at my calling card. "I guess that is you?"

I nod. "It is."

"What do you want to know?"

"I am working with the Metropolitan Police and Inspector Abberline specifically to help catch the Ripper. I have been given a copy of your testimony from the inquisition, but is there anything you can add? Perhaps something you may have remembered since then?"

McCarthy takes a deep breath and then looks at Bowyer. "The sight Thomas and I saw that morning..." He shakes his head. "I doubt we will ever get it out of our minds."

Bowyer nods.

"All this talk of the Ripper being a man, it is false I tell you. What I saw that morning was the work of the devil."

Bowyer says, "No man in his right mind could do such a thing to another human being."

McCarthy continues. "The Whitechapel murders have been the main focus of most conversations around here, but I declare to God the Almighty, I never expected to see such a sight. The whole scene was more than I could ever describe. and I pray I never lay my eyes on anything like that again."

I bow my head at the thought. *You can do this, Jax. Due diligence will get your killer. Avenge Marie's death and all those other women who were unjustly murdered.* I nod as if to answer my own thoughts. "How long did Miss Kelly and Joe Barnett live at 13 Miller's Court?"

"About ten months."

"And what did they pay you for rent and how often?"

"They paid by the week, four pence a week."

I hesitate and then ask, "I understand that you sent Mr. Bowyer to collect the rent that day. Was it in arrears?"

"Yes, they owed twenty-nine shillings."

I find it odd that a landlord would allow the rent to get this far behind. Why did he decide to suddenly collect it? "Mr. McCarthy, what possessed you to collect the rent on that particular day?"

He clears his throat. "Well, they had accumulated quite a bit of rent like I had said."

"Why did you allow so much to accumulate?"

He sits in the chair behind the counter and sighs. "I guess it is going to come out eventually." He looks at Bowyer and says, "Thomas, run down to the market and pick up some apples for Mrs. McCarthy. She is making an apple pie today."

Thomas nods and gets up and leaves.

McCarthy looks back at me and says, "I am a very happily married man, Mr. Kent, but sometimes... well, I am sure you know a wife is not always in the mood, and I am then forced to find comfort elsewhere."

"For some men, Mr. McCarthy." I had to point out that not all men disregard their wedding vows.

He looks down and then back at me. "Of course," he says ashamed. He then continues. "Marie and I had an agreement. I would allow the rent to accumulate for a short time and she, um, she..."

I finish his thought. "She would grant you sexual favors?"

He fidgets. "Yes."

"Did you tell this to the police?"

He shakes his head.

"How long had this been going on?"

"It started about a month after she and Barnett moved in."

"Did Barnett know?"

"No, he would have killed me."

I can't help the chuckle that escapes me. "Indeed he would have." I begin to pace. "But, Mr. McCarthy, your confession still does not tell my why you collected on the ninth of November. Most landlords collect at the beginning of the week or month. Why would you pick a Friday and collect at the end of the week?"

"Because I visited Miss Kelly the night she died, and she refused me. Told me she was in love and leaving Whitechapel. She said her lover was rich and he would be there in the morning to pay her rent. She was drunk, and I did not believe her. She was a very quiet woman for the most part, except when she was drunk. I left her room afterward and could hear her singing into the night as I made my way back to the shop."

"Singing? What was she singing?" I find this odd. When Marie fled Jasper, she was terrified for her life and believed I was a murderer. Then, as the night progressed, she tells another man no because she is in love and then she is singing as if not to have a care in the world. It does not add up unless it was the drink.

"A Violet from Mother's Grave." As he utters the words, a chill goes up my spine. I remember Ginny is waiting, and I really do not think I am going to get any more information out of Mr. McCarthy today. "Well, Mr. McCarthy, thank you for speaking with me today. You have my card. If you think of anything more, please do not hesitate to call on me."

He holds the card up. "I sure will, Mr. Kent."

I turn and walk out, making my way back toward my carriage. The song plays in my mind.

> But while life does remain in memoriam, I'll retain this small violet I pluck'd from Mother's grave.
> Only a violet I pluck'd when but a boy, and oft' times when I'm sad at heart this flower has giv'n me joy. So while life does remain in memoriam, I'll retain the small violet I pluck'd from Mother's grave.[iii]

When I get to the carriage, I am pleased to see that Ginny is waiting inside. I step in. "I'm so sorry, my dear. That took longer than I expected. Well shall get you back to Madame Grace now."

"I like you," she says as she looks up at me with her big blue eyes. "You talk nice and have pretty horses."

I chuckle. "Well, young lady, I like you too."

We make our way down Dorsett Street to Commercial Road and pull up in front of Madame Grace's. Carlton steps down and opens my door. I step out and go around and open the door for Ginny, holding out my hand.

"My lady," I say to her with a bow.

She smiles wide. Her eyes sparkle with delight as she takes my hand and steps down from the carriage.

"I could get used to this," she says as we walk to the door.

Her words cause me to falter in my step.

"Are you all right, sir?" she asks, still holding my hand.

"Yes, sweetheart, I am." I do not tell her I have heard those words before. Marie had said them to me many times, and every time she said them, it made me want to shower her with luxuries. And though I will never get to spoil Marie, I have Ginny whom I can spoil to my heart's content.

When we get to the door, I kneel in front of Ginny. "Do you like living here?"

"Yes. I have no other place to live," she says innocently.

"Tell me then. If you had another place to live, would you want to leave here?"

She giggles. "Well, that depends on where."

I can't help but laugh myself. I did not specify that the other place to live would be better or worse. She will not commit to something if it is worse. Again, she reminds me of Marie.

"Good answer. What if I told you this place was much better than Madame's place? You would have your own room, lots of toys to play with, and maybe even a pony of your own. Would you like that?"

"Oh!" She squeals. "I would!"

I notice the buttons on her coat are all buttoned wrong, and I work to fix them. "Let this be our little secret for now. I will talk to Madame and see what I can work out."

She wraps her arms around my neck. "I love you." With her arms still wrapped around me, she says, "What is your name?"

The full-blown belly laugh that comes from me feels so good. It has been days since I laughed—I mean really laughed. This child is enchanting. "It is Jackson Kent, but you can call me Jax."

"I love you, Jax," she says and kisses me on the cheek, and my heart swells.

CHAPTER NINE

Ginny turns toward the door and opens it. As she steps inside, she checks to make sure I am behind her. One of the ladies in the main room, who is scantily dressed, approaches Ginny. "Where have you been, young lady?" she scolds.

"I went to Marie's just like Madame said, but then I met Jax and I have been with him." She looks up at me proudly as the prostitute looks me over warily.

"Well, Madame is waiting for you." She gestures up the stairs. "You better get a move on."

Ginny looks at me and reaches for my hand. She is afraid to face Madame Grace. Oh Lord, please tell me this child is not physically abused as well. We make our way up the stairs and proceed to Madame Grace's office. I knock on the door, and from the other side, she says, "Enter."

Ginny and I walk in, and Madame gives us both the oddest look. I even think Ginny is surprised.

"Well, Mr. Kent, you were the last person I expected to see just now."

"Forgive the intrusion, Madame, but I ran into Ginny in Miller's Court earlier and insisted that she wait for me and I bring her back to you. It was getting late in the afternoon and not a place for a child to be roaming the streets on her own, do you not agree?"

"Certainly," she replies and then looks at Ginny. "Did you get the shawl?"

"I did!" she replies proudly, handing the red shawl to Madame Grace.

"Very good child. Now run along. I need to speak with Mr. Kent."

Ginny runs over to me and gives me another hug. "See you soon, Jax."

"Ginny!" Madame Grace yells. "Apologize at once for being so disrespectful to Mr. Kent!"

Ginny stops at the door and turns toward me, looking sad. Before she can say anything, I intervene.

"Madame Grace, it is me who told Ginny she could call me Jax." I touch Ginny's cheek. "Please do not scold her for something I told her was acceptable."

Looking annoyed, she replies, "Very well then." She gestures for the child to leave, and Ginny winks at me and walks out the door. "So, Mr. Kent, what can I do for you?"

"I'll get to the point, Madame Grace. Which one of your girls is Ginny's mother?"

She stands. "Ginny's mother has died, Mr. Kent. I am her mother now."

"And is this a position you enjoy?"

"Not particularly, but what choice do I have?"

"Let me take Ginny. I will raise her as if she were my own daughter."

Madame Grace laughs. "You can't be serious?"

Surprised by her laughter, I say, "I am very serious, I assure you."

She walks around her desk. "Oh the irony of it all." She continues to laugh.

"What? What?"

"Oh, Mr. Kent, I am astonished that you have not figured it out yet."

I'm still lost. "What? What should I have figured out?"

She walks to the door and opens it to call for the child. "Ginny. Ginny. Someone please send Ginny to my office." She leaves the door open and goes back to her desk and sits.

A few minutes go by and Ginny comes rushing into the office, closing the door behind her. "Yes, ma'am?"

"Ginny, go and stand in front of Mr. Kent." She then turns toward me. "Mr. Kent, look at her. Take a good close look at her."

I look at the child standing before me. She has blonde curls and deep blue eyes. She smiles at me, and my heart melts. And that is when I see it. The same smile. The same eyes. The same hair. The same turned-up nose. *Oh my God!*

I look at Madame Grace with tears in my eyes. "Is she?"

She nods. "Ginny, you may go now." She turns back toward me. "Yes, Mr. Kent, she is Marie's daughter."

"Why did you not tell me before?"

She smirks, "Honestly, I thought you figured it out when you were here the other day. Their resemblance is uncanny, so I truly did not think I would have to tell you. Then when you asked about her, I just assumed you knew."

"I have been so wrapped up in finding Marie's killer, I never really looked at her closely until now." I wipe the tears from my cheeks. "She does not refer to Marie as her mother?"

"No, she wouldn't. She was a little over two years old when Marie came here. She dropped her with me and instructed me to take care of her. She was going to France. That is when she left to go with Carlisle Hamilton. Six months later when she returned, she paid the child no mind and never acknowledged her as her own."

I shake my head. "I find that so hard to believe. The Marie I knew was kind and caring. She would never abandon a child, especially her own."

"Oh, Mr. Kent, Marie was a paid actress. All my girls are. They are whatever their john wants them to be."

I lean back in the chair. "I don't believe that."

"Mr. Kent, do not be naïve. Do you really believe you were special to her? Perhaps you were more in the end, but not at first. You were rent and food and that is all."

I think about her words. She is right. I started out as a meal ticket to Marie. I was a roof over her head and a hot meal every day.

Madame Grace continues. "Marie was an opportunist, Mr. Kent. She used every man she ever encountered, and frankly I am not surprised, however how sad it is, that she is dead."

"You are right, but I know things changed for us toward the end." It angers me how she brushes off our relationship like I was just another client for her, but her opinion really does not matter. I know what we had, and I will treasure those happy memories for as long as I live.

"Perhaps. I hope so, if it will help you sleep at night."

I lean forward and rest my elbows onto the tops of my thighs. "So about the child? Who is her father? Do you know?"

"Marie's husband. When he died and she left Cardiff, she tried to find other work but nothing worked out. She spent some time in the West End and ended up working in a brothel there. That is where she met Carlisle Hamilton. Carlisle was so taken with her and requested her on every occasion. He was needy and possessive, and so Marie and Ginny left, which is when she came to me. She worked for me for a couple of months until Carlisle found her. He offered her the world, including Paris, so she agreed. Paris was no place for a child, so she left her with me and never looked back at her."

"What about when she returned?"

"Like I said, six months later she returned. She treated the child as if she were a stranger."

"Poor Ginny."

"I have done what I could for her, Mr. Kent. I am not a wealthy woman, but I do make a good living from my girls. Ginny has not gone without. I can assure you that."

I nod. "I can see that for myself, but I gather her being here is not ideal for you?"

"Mr. Kent, the last thing I need is a child around here." She stands and walks around to the front of her desk. "Do not misunderstand me. I love the child. And she helps out a lot around here, but let's be honest, shall we? This is no place for a child."

"No, it is not. Not to mention the things I could provide for her."

"Exactly."

I stand. "So we are in agreement? The child will come and live with me?"

"Agreed. You may take her tonight if you wish."

I think about that for a minute. *No, not tonight.* "Madame, I should like to wait until this business with the Ripper is settled. There is a good possibility that when the Ripper realizes I am on his tail, I could be in danger. If Ginny is with me, it can put her in harm's way. You and I both would not want that for her. If she stays with you for the time being, she is a nobody in his eyes and that makes her safe."

She nods. "I understand completely." She walks to the door and places her hand on the knob. "Would you like to tell her now or wait?"

"I've already made promises to her, so I will need to explain to her why she cannot come with me now, and I would like to say good-bye to her."

"Of course." She turns the knob and opens the door. To her surprise, Ginny is standing outside her door. "My Goodness, Ginny. Were you eavesdropping?"

She shakes her head vehemently. "No, ma'am. I was just coming up to let you know Mr. Xavier was here."

"Thank you, child. Please come in for a minute." Ginny walks in and stands next to me. "Mr. Kent is getting ready to leave and would like to say good-bye to you."

She looks at me and she looks like she is about to cry. "Mr. Kent? I thought..."

"Oh, sweetheart, I swear everything I promised you will come true. You just have to stay here for some time until I can, uh, get things prepared for you."

"Do you promise?" She is on the verge of a full blown-out cry and is trying very hard to hold it in.

I pull her into a hug.

"Mr. Kent, you will come back for me, right?"

I pull her out of the hug and stand her in front of me, taking out my handkerchief. I gently wipe her tears. "Now you listen to me, young lady. When I make a promise, I keep it. I swear to you I will come back for you. You will come to live with me, and I promise," I say, emphasizing the word, "*promise* I will buy you a pony."

She looks at me as more tears fall down her cheeks.

"Do you believe me?"

"Yes, I do."

"Good, now give me a hug and I will see you soon."

She wraps her little arms around my neck and squeezes tight. She whispers, "Please do not forget me."

I squeeze her and then kiss her hair. Even before I knew who she was, I was not able to forget her. There is no way now, knowing she is Marie's, that I will leave her here.

She kisses me on the cheek and turns to leave. When she closes the door behind her, Madame Grace turns my direction.

"Mr. Kent, and what do I tell her if you do not survive this mission of yours?"

"Madame Grace, you will not have to worry about it. I will survive. I have something to live for. And as far as the Ripper is concerned, the world will have one less sadistic murderer. That I can guarantee."

"Very well, Mr. Kent. I wish you all the best."

"Oh, I almost forgot." I reach into my pocket and pull out some money, then hand it to Madame Grace. "Would you have some time to take Ginny shopping? She will need some new dresses."

"Of course, Mr. Kent. I could find some time late tomorrow morning if that works for you?"

"Yes, I will have my driver pick you both up outside the brothel at half past eleven." I turn toward the door. "I don't carry a lot of money with me, but Jasper, my driver, will have access to my accounts in the shops in the West End." I reach for the knob but turn back toward Madame Grace. "Whatever she wants, and be sure to get yourself something for your trouble."

"Mr. Kent, it is no trouble at all. I am happy the child will have a better life. And thank you."

"I shall be in touch. Take good care of my angel, Madame Grace."

"I will, Mr. Kent. I promise," she says as I step out of her office.

I make my way downstairs and out the door where Carlton, just like always, is patiently—and I might add nervously—waiting out front. I chuckle. He really dislikes this place. My spirits are lighter than they have been in days. I'm actually smiling as I step into the carriage. Ginny and the prospect of raising her has brought new meaning to my life.

As Carlton drives off, I think about all I have lost: Charlotte, my unborn child, Marie... Did it all happen for a reason? Did I suffer all so Ginny and I could be happy? And then, it is as if my eyes have been opened for the first time and I see my future before me. Yes. The answer to all my questions is yes. If my past had been different. there is a definite possibility I would not have encountered Ginny. I take a deep breath and sigh. For the first time in a long time, peace washes over me.

I think I shall spend the day at White's tomorrow. It has been a long time since I have been there.

CHAPTER TEN

The next day I breakfast, luncheon, and dine at White's. It has been months since I have spent the afternoon amongst the elite gentlemen of London, and I find I have missed it. White's provides a multitude of activities beyond meals. There are billiards, cards, plenty to drink, and good company. Many of my Eton school chums spend their days at White's. I have spent my afternoon catching up and all that applies.

While sitting at one of the tables, reading the latest news, I hear: "Jackson Kent!"

I lower my newspaper to see who is addressing me.

I put my paper on the table and stand. "Lord Edwards!" I greet happily. Oliver Edwards and I attended Eton and were the closest of friends back in the day. And I have to say I am a bit embarrassed to admit that we were often in trouble and spent many hours in the headmaster's office. "It has been a while." I put my hand out, and he shakes it eagerly.

"Oh my word, Jax, call me Oliver. We go back way too far for formalities. And yes, it has been some time. How have you been, old friend?"

"Doing well, Oliver." I gesture toward the chair across from the one I was just sitting in. "Join me, please."

He adjusts his waistcoat and sits. After reaching into his pocket, he pulls out two cigars and hands one to me. "Cigar?"

I take it. "Yes, thank you."

We light our cigars and spend the next several hours catching up. Many sentences started with "Do you remember when..." or "How could we have been so awful..."

"It's a wonder we never got expelled."

We laugh, and before we know it, time has gotten away from us. A tall slender man walks in and approaches Oliver. "Lord Howard, you asked me to fetch you when the hour approached ten."

He moves to stand. "Indeed, Carlisle, I did. Thank you."

I stand as well, and we shake hands.

"It has been so good catching up, Jax. We should not be such strangers."

"Agreed. I am looking forward to brighter days ahead, and I intend to spend more time here. I'm sure we will cross paths."

"Oh, I'm counting on it." He tips his hat and turns and walks away, Carlisle following behind him. As I watch them walk out the door, a cold chill washes over me. *Carlisle. Could that man be Carlisle Hamilton?* I shake my head. Of course not, Jax. There are thousands of men in England named Carlisle.

For the remainder of the night, I cannot shake the feeling I had seen the Ripper tonight. At one in the morning, I decide I have had enough of billiards and drink and call for my coat. After saying my good-byes to the gentlemen with me, I then make my way toward the door. I think back to the descriptions in the testimonies of the men seen with Marie. All were pretty much the same: short and stout with a bushy mustache that curled at the ends. This man was tall and slender, and therefore I convince myself he is not the Ripper.

I step down from the stoop and walk toward my carriage. Carlton is waiting as usual. I step into the carriage, and the cold chill returns. I look around me and get the distinct feeling I am being watched. I step back down from the carriage and scan my surroundings.

"Sir?" Carlton asks. "Is something wrong?"

I turn toward him and shake my head. "No, Carlton, everything is fine." I step back up into the carriage, chalking the chill to the weather. Then I realize it is unseasonably pleasant for this time of year and there is no reason to be chilled. Carlton steers us toward home, and the whole time I can't help looking behind to see if we are being followed.

We arrive back at the house, and the uneasy feeling has not subsided. This evening was so nice, catching up with old friends, until Oliver's driver approached. I had completely forgotten about the Ripper, Marie, and all the death, but when Carlisle arrived, it all came back with a vengeance. I am convinced there is a connection; I felt it. I am also convinced I was being watched, but by whom? Could it have been the Ripper himself? It has not escaped me that he knows me, and by now, he probably knows I am hunting him. It was smart to leave Ginny with Madame Grace. I am closing in on him. I don't know how or when, but I will meet him real soon, and God help him when I do.

***

Several days later, I find myself back at White's. Something keeps nagging at me that I am missing clues here. I spend another afternoon, and to my surprise, Lord Howard returns. He joins me and offers me another cigar.

"Good to see you, Jax. I told you we would run into each other again."

"Oliver," I greet. "It has been really nice seeing you after all this time." We settle into a casual banter, talking about the prime minister and the queen. We have differing opinions on such matters. It is so important to not discuss politics with friends.

Oliver takes a hit from his cigar. "So, Jax, what do you make of the heinous murders in Whitechapel?"

My chest tightens. I cannot talk about it without giving away my connection, and right now, I prefer I remain removed from them in the eyes of my friends.

I wave my hand in an attempt to brush off his question. "Heinous indeed. So unfortunate." I shake my head in disgust. I remain brief in the hopes he will take my words at face value and move on to another topic of discussion, but he does not.

"I hear they have several suspects, including the prince of Wales."

"I did hear that." Again I keep it vague and do not elaborate on anything that would encourage the conversation.

He leans forward. "Come on, old friend, you must have an idea of who the killer might be." He looks at me intently, and I find that his gaze makes me uncomfortable.

I need to pull myself together, and when I do, I reply, "I do not. To be honest, I really have not given it much thought." I chuckle a nervous laugh. "After all, I am not a detective or inspector. I will leave that up to the professionals."

Oliver laughs.

I decide to turn the conversation around. "Oliver, how long has Carlisle been working for you?" I realize this question is odd, so I back it up by saying, "I'm in need of a new driver and was wondering if perhaps he might have some contacts or friends he could recommend." It's not true, but it makes the question viable and ensures that I appear as though I am fishing for information.

"He's been with me for quite some time now. Three or four years, I would guess." He waves his hand in the air. "I truly do not keep up with such things." He leans back in his chair. "But I can ask him for you."

"Thank you, I would appreciate that." Just then, Carlisle walks in and I eye him warily. No, he definitely does not fit the description of the witnesses.

He addresses Oliver. "Sir, I have some errands to run for Hamilton. Will you be here a while?"

Hamilton? Carlisle? Carlisle Hamilton? But Carlisle Hamilton is one person, and the references here are obviously two different people. Carlisle is his driver and Hamilton must be his butler or manservant. He must be a member of Oliver's household. It is just a coincidence.

Oliver grins and says, "Actually, Carlisle, I need to go." He gets up and turns toward me. "Until the next time, Jax."

I nod. He quickly turns, and as I watch him leave, I know.

My chest tightens, and my throat goes dry. My heart begins to race, and the hair on my arms and neck begin to prickle. George Hutchinson's words come back to me.

> *"He was pale with a slight mustache turned up at the corners. His hair was dark. He was wearing a soft felt hat pulled down over his eyes, a long dark coat trimmed in astrakhan collar and cuffs, dark trousers, and a white collar with a black necktie fixed with a horseshoe pin. There was a massive gold chain in his waistcoat with a large seal. A red stone was hanging from it. He carried kid gloves in one hand and, like I said, a small package or parcel in the other. I would guess him to be five six or five seven, and I would estimate he is around thirty-five or thirty-six years old."*

And then Sarah Lewis...

> *I remember him clearly. He was short, pale faced with a black mustache. The bag he carried was about nine inches to a foot long. He wore a round high hat and a brownish long overcoat with a short black coat underneath. He wore pepper and salt trousers.*

I know who the Ripper is.

CHAPTER ELEVEN

November 19, 1888

    Today is Marie's funeral. Her remains will finally be laid to rest. When the horrifying facts of her death were revealed to the public, an outpour of sympathy resulted but no family members came forward. So I paid for the funeral expenses as I wanted Marie to have a proper burial.

    I know Fred had been searching for any of Marie's family but had no luck last I spoke to him. He does not know about Ginny, and I prefer to keep it that way. The last thing I want to do is to make the child a target. I had thought about bringing her, because someday I intend to tell her about her mother, but right now she does not remember Marie being her mother. She would not understand the reasoning as to why I would want her here, and I do not intend to explain it to her until she is older. And, it would make a statement that I am connected to her somehow. He is watching, and that is the last thing I want him to know. Besides, this would just scare her too. She is already bothered by Marie's murder; there is no reason to torment the child further.

    I arranged for a polished oak-and-elm coffin with metal fittings and a brass coffin plate that read: *Marie Jeanette Kelly, died 9th November 1888, aged 25* years. There were also to be two wreaths of artificial flowers and a cross made of heartseed to be placed on the coffin. An open hearse drawn by two horses followed by two mourning carriages would take the coffin from Shoreditch mortuary to St. Patrick's Catholic Cemetery in Leytonstone.

Barnett, McCarthy, and I worked together to ensure she was buried according to the traditions of the Roman Catholic Church. Marie never indicated to me she was a practicing Catholic, but both Barnett and McCarthy insisted she was. They felt it would be important to her, and so I agreed.

I arrive at Shoreditch mortuary and am surprised by the enormous crowd completely blocking the public thoroughfare gathered outside at this early hour. I notice several police constables placed around the area to keep order and protect the property.

At noon, the lone bell of St. Leonard's begins to toll. The coffin appears at the main gates of St. Leonard's, borne on the shoulders of four men. Many of the onlookers surge forward in an effort to touch the coffin as it passes them. Women with tears streaming down their faces are screaming, "God forgive her!" while every man removes his hat in respect for my love. The emotion emanating from the crowd is overwhelming and completely unconstrained.

I watch as the coffin that holds the remains of my love is loaded onto the hearse while two the two mourning carriages pull up behind it. Joseph Barnett, a woman representing John McCarthy and Madame Grace, and I enter the first carriage. The second carriage holds five women who gave testimony at the inquest, including Sarah Lewis. Carlton brings my carriage up behind.

After a tremendous struggle with the crowds, the open hearse—with the coffin fully exposed to view—sets off at a very slow pace, followed by the mourning carriages and Carlton. The crowd begins to move simultaneously. The distance from St. Leonard's to the cemetery is approximately six miles. As the procession makes its way along Whitechapel Road, I notice the street is full of onlookers on both sides to pay their respects to Marie. We arrive at the cemetery at approximately two o'clock.

Father Columban, Order of St. France meets us at the door of the small St. Patrick chapel. The coffin is then removed from the hearse and carried to the open grave in the northeastern corner listed as no. 16, row 67.

Joseph Barnett, the weeping women from the mourning carriages, and I kneel by the gravesite while Father Columban reads the service. I notice there is a crowd that has gathered outside the locked gates while the service is taking place. The service is short, and when Father Columban concludes the service, the men who place the coffin into the ground struggle from its weight. I cannot help thinking to myself, *death cannot kill what never dies*. Almost everyone leaves, but I find I cannot move while the dirt is shoveled onto Marie's coffin. I stay until the coffin is completely covered. My love is finally at peace. I make my way to my carriage.

The death certificate names her as Marie Jeanette Kelly, which is also noted on her marker. I am pleased to see the additional words I had requested are noted on the marker as well.

None but the lonely hearts can know my sadness
Love Lives Forever

I find comfort in the words Marie and I spoke in her room after her murder. She knows I loved her dearly, and she knows our love will live on forever. We leave the cemetery, and I instruct Carlton to return home. I have no desire to be out any more today and plan on spending a quiet afternoon at home.

Once home, I have my supper and retire to my study. As I'm lighting a cigar, I think about all I have discovered over the course of the last ten days. I think about Ginny, and I think about the Ripper.

Now that I know who the Ripper is, the only question remaining is if I go after him or if he will come for me. Unfortunately, it does not take me long to know he will come for me. This has to be on his terms, when he is good and ready. He thinks he knows me, but he does not. He has always underestimated me, and over the years, I'd think he would have learned. Unfortunately for him, he did not.

***

Several days pass, and I know he is watching my every move. He has been watching me from the beginning. I just did not know it until recently. I even sensed his presence at the service, but I did not see him. I debate on whether to involve Fred, but this is too personal. I will explain everything to Fred after the Ripper is dead.

I am constantly on guard, waiting for him to make contact. I know he will and that he is dragging this out on purpose. He wants to catch me unprepared, but he will not. I am ready and waiting ever so patiently.

It has been a fortnight since I was last at White's. I'm sitting in my study when Rothschild comes in. "Excuse the intrusion, sir, but this letter arrived for you just now." He hands it to me, and I open it. It is from Madame Grace.

I must see you right away.
Please come to my office as soon as possible
Yours,
Madame Grace

I fold the paper up and look at Rothschild. "Please have Carlton prepare the carriage. We need to leave immediately."

The carriage is prepared in record time, and within fifteen minutes, we are on our way to Whitechapel and Madame Grace's fine establishment. When we arrive, I do not even wait for Carlton to open my door. I rush out and to the brothel. Walking inside, I do not even wait to be announced and make my way to her office.

I knock.

"Enter," she states.

I step inside, and Madame Grace looks relieved to see me. "I just got your note."

"Thank you for coming so quickly, Mr. Kent." She takes a piece of paper from her desk drawer and walks around the desk to hand it to me. "This was given to Ginny yesterday when she was returning from the market. The man told her to give it to me, but it is addressed to you."

I take the piece of paper and open it. My heart drops to the floor as I realize my efforts to hide Ginny from him have failed. He knows who she is, and he knows her connection to me. My stomach turns into knots. He was close enough to Ginny to give her this note. She spoke with him. He could have easily taken her, but he didn't. *Why?* I do not need to know why at the moment, and I thank the good Lord he left her alone.

The note reads:

13 Miller's Court
The evening of 4 December, 10 o'clock
I'll be waiting

That is tonight. Well, it is about time. I look at the handwriting closely. It is in his signature red ink, and it really does resemble my own. I turn toward Madame Grace.

"I need your help with something. Can you acquire for me a knife and perhaps a pistol? I will need it before tonight."

"Mr. Kent?" she questions.

"It ends tonight, Madame."

"But, Mr. Kent, should you not have backup? You should not face this mad man alone."

"Thank you for your concern. I will be all right. I know who the Ripper is. I have known for a couple of weeks. I have just been waiting for him to make contact and now he has. It has to be the two of us."

"I see. And what about Ginny?" she asks.

"Keep her safe. I will come for her in the morning. I promise."

She walks to the door. "Wait here. I will see what I can do about getting you some weapons."

I sit and wait as she closes the door behind her. I pull the note back out of my pocket and open it again. This time, however, when I read his words, I hear his voice. Chills run up and down my spine. My thoughts are interrupted when Madame Grace returns.

She steps into the room and says, handing the pistol to me, "This was all I could find." It's a flintlock, and I am pleased.

"This will do nicely, Madame. It is small enough to conceal." I am sure the gun is the way to go because I do not believe the Ripper likes to use a gun. He would have in the past. No, he likes to carve his victims. "Did you find a knife?"

She hands me a knife. It is bigger than the pistol with a scary jagged edge. It makes me wonder why she would have such things, but I assume in her line of work, she has to protect herself and her girls. It makes sense. "That will do just fine, thank you." I take the knife from her.

"So what now, Mr. Kent?"

"We wait." I pause and then say, "I hope you do not mind if I wait here for a bit."

"Of course not. I just wish you would contact the police and not go there alone." She shuffles through some papers on her desk. "Ginny needs you, Mr. Kent. She deserves a good home and a parent. You could make her a true orphan."

"I know what I am doing, Madame. Please do not interfere and contact them."

She shakes her head. "I will not."

"Good."

***

Time passes slowly, and it is finally half past nine. Time to go. I decide to walk to Miller's Court and not involve Carlton. I instruct him to wait. "I do not know how long I will be, Carlton, but I will return."

"But, sir?"

"Carlton, just stay with the carriage. I shall return as soon as I can.

I make my way down Commercial Street and turn down Dorsett. I do not feel as if I am being followed anymore, and I realize it is because he is already there waiting for me. When I get to the entrance of Miller's Court, I pause. Taking a deep breath, I check inside my jacket for the gun. It's tucked safely inside but in a position where I can quickly retrieve it if necessary. The knife is in my hand as I really have no place to hide it, but that is fine. He will ask for it when I enter anyway, and frankly, he can have it. I would rather have the gun.

I walk up to 13 Miller's Court and notice there is a fire blazing in the fireplace. Looking in the window, I see a lit lantern sitting on the table beside the bed. I glance at the table in the middle of the room and see him, his back toward me. I could pull out my pistol right now and shoot him, but I do not.

I need answers.

I step inside.

"You are early, Jax," he says.

"I walk in. I did not know how long it would take."

He does not turn around to face me. "Give me the knife and sit down. We have much to talk about."

I walk around the table, lay the knife on the table, and take the chair across from him. He is in his disguise, and now that he's incognito, I recognize him as the man who stopped me at the House of Lords and asked for directions. But, unfortunately for him, I know what he looks like underneath his disguise. *Oliver Howard.*

"So, Oliver, I assume you are planning to tell me why before you kill me. Am I correct?"

"You were always a to-the-point kind of guy, Jax." He takes off his gloves. "Yes, shall I begin?"

"Please." I feel Marie's presence again, and I wonder if he can feel her too. *He's cunning, Jax, please be careful. Ginny needs you,* she says, and I find comfort to know she is here.

"I met Marie about three years ago, and just like you, I fell in love. She knew me as Carlisle Hamilton. She never knew my real name." He sighs. "She was everything I had dreamed of in a woman, and I wanted her for my own. She was a prostitute in the West End, in a rather upscale brothel. I frequented it often, and she was my only girl. Our relationship got very serious rather quickly, and I proposed marriage. She got scared and ran." He stands to pace the room.

I'm fine with his pacing as long as he does not get behind me. I follow him with my eyes around the room.

He laughs. "Smart man, Jackson. You should always keep your eyes on me." He laughs some more and then continues. "She fled to Madame Grace with the child."

So he has known about Ginny since the beginning.

"When she got settled a few days later, I approached her. I apologized for rushing things between us and asked her to go away with me on an extended trip to Paris. She was elated as she had never been to Paris, and the thought excited her." He stops pacing and turns toward me. "You see, Jax, I had plans for her in Paris. I was going to make her love me, and we were going to be married." He resumes his pacing. "But you know what they say about the best laid plans. She started stealing from me, and after about a month in France, she ran off."

"Why is that? What was she so afraid of?"

"You mean you do not know, Jax? She did not tell you?"

"No, she did not. She just said she left you."

"I am a sadist, Jackson. I enjoy inflicting pain on others, especially women. I find it highly arousing to see a woman's flesh red and swollen from the pain I inflict. Marie was no exception. She was whipped, starved, humiliated, and raped on a daily basis. She was caged at times, and spent most of her time on her knees."

His words sicken me. I almost gag as my stomach churns. I clear my throat in an attempt to stifle the bile rising in my throat. He tortured her, abused her, and raped her. No wonder she ran. "And you wonder why she left you? I should think it is pretty clear."

He walks to the table and slams his hand down. "Enough!" He continues to the door and turns his back toward me. "She thanked me for every punishment. She enjoyed it, Jax. She craved it." He turns. "That is what made her so perfect for me."

"Well you are right about one thing, Oliver. You are a sadist."

He laughs.

"So tell me, why? I mean, I understand you wanted Marie, but why kill all those women and kill her? Why destroy so many lives?"

"That is easy to explain. At first, the plan was to show her it was dangerous to be on the streets and that she would be safer married to me. But then I learned about Victoria—"

"What does my sister have to do with all of this?"

"I found out about your sister and her addiction. We may have been friends at Eton, Jax, but I truly hated you. I may have had the title, but you had the charm, charisma, and good looks. You had everything I wanted." He rakes his hands through his hair. "I was so fucking jealous of you.

"When I befriended your sister, I used her as a pawn to draw you in." He sits back down. "Do you truly believe you met Marie by chance the night Polly Nichols was murdered? Do you believe it was coincidental that on the nights of the murders, you were not at home?" He laughs again. "And there is the *Dear Boss* letter, but I believe you have already figured that out."

He leans back comfortably. "It was all orchestrated by me. I was the puppet master pulling the strings, and you, Marie, and your dear sister all had a part to play." He sighs and then says, "I never thought I would enjoy killing all those women, but when you are a sadist like me, well... I do not think I really need to explain myself, now do I?" He takes out his knife and lays it on the table. Does he really believe I am just going to let him kill me, right here in the same place he killed Marie? His hand is resting on the knife.

Suddenly, there is a lot of commotion outside. Without thinking, he turns to look out the window and I make my move.

I stand and quickly pull the Flintlock from my pocket. While his head is still turned trying to figure out what is going on outside, I cock the pistol and hold it to his temple, pushing the knife away with my other hand. "Who is the puppet master now, Oliver?" I ask.

He stays in position, facing his head to the window, as the door to 13 Miller's Court is broken in. Fred and the boys from H Division come in, guns cocked and ready. I keep the gun held to Oliver's head.

"Fred, meet Jack the Ripper. Also known as Lord Oliver Howard and Carlisle Hamilton."

Fred walks toward him and says to one of his officers, "Cuff him."

Oliver laughs. "Do you all really think I will go quietly?" He quickly turns toward me and reaches for the knife.

I'm still holding the gun on him, but it doesn't deter him. He flays the knife at me, and without thinking, I fire the pistol. The bullet enters his temple and blood flows from his mouth as his head drops to the table.

Fred grabs his wrist and checks for a pulse. "Dead," he says as he drops Oliver's wrist onto the table. He turns toward me. "You have killed the Ripper, Jax."

"I guess I have."

"Why the fuck did you not tell me about tonight?" he yells.

"I had to do this on my own." I run my fingers through my hair. "How did you know?"

"Madame Grace came down to the station and told us she thought there might be trouble here tonight."

I smirk. Of course she did.

"Do you know him?" Fred asks.

I nod, "Yes, Oliver Howard."

Fred looks at me surprised, "Oliver Howard? The Earl of Carlisle?" I nod.

He shakes his head, "Unfortunately, you know we cannot publicize this. The world cannot know that the Earl of Carlisle is the heinous killer that has terrorized Whitechapel."

"I understand." I lay the pistol on the table and turn back toward Fred. "May I go?"

"Yes, we do not want you involved in this either, Jax. No need to tarnish your good name by association."

I nod. "Thank you, I appreciate that." It is common for titled members to be shielded from the law, even murder. Although I appreciate the protection for myself, there is a part of me that wants the world to know what this man has done. His son will become Earl, and I can only hope and pray he is nothing like his father.

"You need to be commended, Jackson. The reign of terror has ended thanks to you."

I walk toward the doorway shaking my head. "This time. There will always be another sick bastard who will do the same. I pray it does not happen again in my lifetime."

"Take care of yourself, Jackson," he says as I step into the doorway.

Before I step out, Marie speaks to me one last time. *Thank you, Jax.*

Epilogue

Four years later ...

I sit in St. James Park and watch my ten-year-old daughter, Ginny, chase a butterfly. She has been with me now for quite some time, and as she gets older, she looks more and more like her mother.

"Father, is the butterfly not the prettiest thing you have ever seen?" She sings. It took her some time to call me Father, but when she finally did, it rolled off her tongue as if it were the most natural thing in the world.

"Not quite, my child, for you are by far the prettiest and most precious thing I have ever seen." I smile at her as she frolics about. She does not have a care in the world, and I would not want it any other way. She seems to have forgotten her humble beginnings and the horrors that surrounded her life.

Right after I left Marie's flat the night I killed Oliver Howard, I headed straight to Madame Grace's brothel. I collected Ginny that very night, and she has been with me ever since. I did not have things set up for her yet, but I was not going to leave her in the brothel another day. All the promises I made her I have delivered on—and then some. She will have every opportunity her mother did not have. I'm not ashamed to say I spoil her rotten. It is the one thing giving me joy in this world. It is so gratifying that I can give her so much, and not just material things. She is loved beyond all reason. There is not one thing she wants.

I have not seen nor heard from Victoria since the day Marie and I saw her at Madame Grace's, but Madame Grace gives me regular reports on her and assures me she is doing well. She has not had a drop of opium, to her knowledge, since she has been in her care. Madame Grace checks in on Ginny from time to time as well. Ginny refers to her as her Aunt Grace and is quite fond of her.

I'd like to think that Marie would be pleased Ginny is with me and under my care. I wish for only one thing, which would be that Marie and I could have raised Ginny together. We would have been such a happy family, and I could have spoiled them both to my heart's content. But it will never be. Now that the years have passed, I accept it.

There is not a day that goes by I do not think of my Marie. She will always be in my heart. Her daughter has been the light my life needed after losing Charlotte and my child and then Marie. This adorable creature gives me so much more than I ever could give her. Someday, I may open my heart again to love, maybe not. Right now, all my love is saved for Ginny.

I smile as I continue to watch her play.

The past no longer controls my future.

It no longer has power over me.

I will never forget the horrors I have witnessed.

I will never forget the darkness. I look over at Ginny and remember: she is the light and the future.

I am finally at peace.

The End

Acknowledgements

As always, I would like to thank my friends and family. Without their support, I never would've had the courage and the vision to become a writer.

I would like to thank my husband, Kevin. You've never doubted me or my abilities. All that I am, you let me be. I love you to the moon and back!

Also, I would like to thank the members of my street team, Amy's Amazing Street Girls. You ladies rock my world, and I am so honored to have you all on my side.

I'd also like to thank Maureen Goodwin, Ann Lopez, Nancy George, and Stephanie Nix. Thank you so much for being my BETAs on this book and all your help and promotion throughout the publishing process.

I would also like to thank Alicia Freeman and Monica Diane. Your PR abilities are amazing, and I couldn't ask for two better personal assistants. You ladies are a pleasure to work with, and I could not be more grateful for all that you do for me.

I would like to thank Rebecca Garcia of Dark Wish Designs. Your insightful ideas, creative cover designs, and marketing materials are top notch! Your incredible design talents make this book shine!

I would also like to thank Ellie Augsburger of Creative Digital Studios for the fantastic formatting of this book.

And finally, but definitely not least, I would like to thank Angie Wade of Novel Nurse Editing. It is truly a pleasure working with you. You make the editing process fun!

About the Author

"Face life as you find it-defiantly and unafraid." –Nietzsche

Amy Cecil is a bestselling and award-winning indie author of both historical and contemporary romance. Her penchant for Austen fan fiction won her the title of Favorite Historical Romance Author (2016-2017) while her MC series has won several awards throughout the indie community. Recently, she has expanded her repertoire to the thriller and erotic genres.

For as long as she can remember, Amy always had a book (or two) that she was reading for the love of getting lost within its pages. Amy has been heard to have said, "I've never given much thought to becoming a writer myself until I realized that if I hadn't written my own version of Mr. Darcy, I might have run out of material to read."

And thus, her first novel was born, *A Royal Disposition*. In the words of Miss Austen herself: "I wish as well as everybody else to be perfectly happy; but, like everybody else, it must be in my own way." Mrs. Cecil writes to do just that.

She lives in North Carolina with her husband, Kevin, and their four dogs. When she isn't creating her next masterpiece or traveling the country for book signings, she enjoys spending time with her husband, friends, and of course her fur babies.

In the meantime, she wants to hear from you

Amazon: https://www.amazon.com/Amy-Cecil
Goodreads: https://www.goodreads.com/authoramycecil
Webpage: http://acecil65.wixsite.com/amycecil
Facebook: www.facebook.com/authoramycecil

Amy's Street Team
Amy's Amazing Street Girls

Are you a member of Amy's street team? If not, you should be! We have all kinds of fun with free reads, sneak peeks, exclusives, games and a weekly SWAG BAG giveaway. Join us!!
https://www.facebook.com/groups/20903646918497/

Sign up for Amy's Newsletter and be in the know on all her latest news!
http://eepurl.com/cPYj3b

Want to talk more about Ripper?
Join the spoiler group on FaceBook!!
https://www.facebook.com/groups/1764603363647008/

Amy's Reader/Spoiler Group for the Knights of Silence MC Series:

Love spoiler groups? Then join us for all Knights talk, including character interviews and special events.
https://www.facebook.com/groups/510758405985409/

Other Books by Amy Cecil

HISTORICAL ROMANCE

A Royal Disposition:
myBook.to/ARoyalDisposition

Relentless Considerations:
myBook.to/RelentlessConsiderations

On Stranger Prides
myBook.to/OnStrangerPridesbyAmyCecil

Ripper
mybook.to/ripperbyamycecil

The Man in the Mirror
mybook.to/MirrorbyAmyCecil

Coming 2020
On Familiar Prides

CONTEMPORARY ROMANCES

ICE:
getBook.at/ICEbyAmyCecil

ICE on FIRE:
getBook.at/ICEonFIREbyAmyCecil

Celtic Dragon:
getbook.at/celticdragonbyamycecil

FORGETTING THE ENEMY – *Book 1*
mybook.to/FTEbyAmyCecil

RAW HONEY
mybook.to/RawHoneybyAmyCecil

LOVING THE ENEMY – *Book 2*

Coming 2020
SAINTE

Don't Forget ...

If you've read Mind of a Killer and loved it, then please leave a review. Authors love reading reviews!

REFERENCES

[i] *The London Times, November 9, 1888*

[ii] *National Archives*

[iii] *A Violet from Mother's Grave, Song and Chorus by Will H. Fox. 1881*

Much of the Jack the Ripper historical information, press information, locations, timelines, etc. were found here:
Casebook: Jack the Ripper
http://www.casebook.org
Stephen P. Ryder & Johnno 1996-2018